THE CHILDREN OF LOKI

A Hardboiled Magic Adventure

TODD ALLEN

Indignant Media

CONTENTS

THE GENTRIFIED BODEGA

STUDENT LOANS, PAID IN BLOOD

SURVEILLANCE FROM BEYOND THE VEIL

THE SOUL TARIFF

TERM LIMITS DON'T MATTER
IF YOU HAVE ENOUGH
CHILDREN

Acknowledgments

This story was brought to you in part though the sponsorship of:

- Ted Adams
- Nick Barrucci
- Ian Chung
- Jason Fliegel
- Domenico Tassone
- Greg Weisman

It was originally serialized online in 8 parts from 2016-2017.

For more information on the Hardboiled Magic series, please visit: http://magicdetective.com or

To subscribe to Todd Allen's newsletter: http://eepurl.com/b_3RI5

THE CURSE OF
THE GOAT

The Irrigated Lawn

❧

"The stadium is cursed and it's leaking out into the neighborhood," Alderman Seamus Sheedy was in a state of high anxiety as he walked through his neighborhood with the man in a black suit. "The neighborhood associations are seizing on it. The press can't be far behind. Think of the property values. Think of the votes. This is a disaster and you need to stop it."

"Curses don't usually leak," replied Mister Lewis. "These things have rules that must be followed. You should probably start at the beginning."

Mister Lewis had the official title of "Physics Consultant." The title was a something of an in-joke. His real job was to clean up messes that resulted from unnatural incidents that sprung from outside the laws of physics. Curses fell broadly under that purview and he'd been summoned on a referral.

"It goes back maybe 70 years," explained the

Alderman. "The team wouldn't let a guy into the stadium because he had his pet goat with him. And he put a curse on the stadium. And they never got out of the playoffs since. But this year, they're really good and the curse is leaking out."

"OK. Back up. This wasn't a service goat, just a pet?"

"I don't think they had service goats back then, so I guess it was a pet."

"This curse. Was it on the stadium, the team or the owner?"

"It's just a curse," Alderman Sheedy's voice rose an octave. "But it's always in the stadium. Everybody knows that."

"Okay," Mister Lewis rolled his eyes. "What can you tell me about the man who placed the curse?"

"He was a Greek."

"And..."

"That's it. It was a long time ago and he's dead now. But the team can't hardly get ahead."

"That sounds more like an urban legend than a curse," Mister Lewis said with a note of mild irritation in his voice. "What makes you so sure this is a real thing?"

"Right there's why I'm so sure," Alderman Sheedy pointed up the block to two visibly drunk young men, both of whom had unzipped their flies and were urinating on the lawn in front of an apartment building. "You just watch what happens."

Alderman Sheedy waved his arms wildly as he quickened his pace and stomped towards the buzzed bros.

"Stop that," screeched Alderman Sheedy. "This is not New York. We do not tolerate public urination here."

The buzzed bros ignored him and kept their streams steady.

"See," Alderman Sheedy turned to Mister Lewis. "Tell me this isn't unnatural."

"A couple of drunks ignoring you is hardly," Mister Lewis began.

"It's completely unnatural," Alderman Sheedy interrupted. "I'm Alderman, my father was Alderman and his father was Alderman. This disrespect for bloodlines is unnatural! Keep watching."

So Mister Lewis kept watching and a curious thing happened. The heads of the buzzed bros started to ever so slightly glow.

"It's starting," whispered the Alderman.

The glow grew brighter and the flickering image of a goat's head danced where the drunk's head should have been.

"Stand back and get ready to run," growled Mister Lewis as he stepped in front of the Alderman.

The buzzed bros with goat heads glanced toward Mister Lewis, then at each other. They slowly zipped up, then turned to face their accusers. As Mister Lewis reached his hand into the inner pocket of his suitcoat, the pair bolted into the street.

It was a food truck that hit them, though it was hard to make out the "Gyros A Go Go" logo on the hood with all the blood spatter. The two drunk bros lay dead in the street. While their bodies were mangled, their heads were once more human.

Won't You Be My Neighbor?

The police station wasn't far and a detail showed up to the scene quicker than might be expected, although having an Alderman as a witness didn't slow the response time any. It was agreed not to mention the goat heads to the police. After all, the food truck driver wasn't entirely sure what she'd seen. Having an Alderman as a witness was also very handy for ensuring Mister Lewis was not officially there at the time of the... accident.

"Hello little cousin," spoke a woman so old her actual age was an afterthought. Alderman Sheedy had not heard her approach and he jumped a little at the sound of her voice. "I see the rabble has been at it again. I'm used to these hooligans making a mess of the neighborhood, but not a mess in the middle of the street. Someone needs to hose it down before the blood settles in."

"As soon as the police finish up, Mrs. Gudrun," the

Alderman stammered. "We'll get the bodies moved and the blood cleaned up. It will all be gone before the odor sets in."

Alderman Sheedy shrank back a little. He'd caught the gaze of the wizened old men who stood behind Gudrun, flanking her like a military escort. It was not the sort of gaze that made one think of tolerance and respect.

"Oh, we're used to those drunks leaving odors behind," Mrs. Gudrun snarled. "It's easier to wash the contents of their stomachs off the pavement than it is to wash it off of my lawn. The only difference I see this time is it's exploding out their stomach wall instead of erupting from their mouth. Weak men overcome by weak drink."

Mister Lewis managed to keep it to only a faint smile as Alderman Sheedy started a full-fledged cringe.

"This used to be a nice neighborhood before baseball took it over," Mrs. Gudrun began to preach with the bile usually reserved for a closeted preacher lecturing about purity. "Now it's loud hooligans who can't hold their liquor. They water our lawns with their salted streams. They fall down like those two and block traffic. This has to stop. No more baseball."

"You know I can't do that," the Alderman was halfway to a whisper. "There's a large tax base that comes with the stadium and the taverns. It's an entertainment district. There have always been beer vendors in the stands and bars around the ballpark."

"Some of us remember when it was quiet," barked Mrs. Gudrun. "No more renovation. No more construction. Your night games and bright lights were bad enough, we don't need more congestion around here. They threatened to build a new park in the suburbs. Send them on their way."

"The city is in no position to turn away taxable revenue..."

"Then let these ne'er do wells watch the other stick ball team on the other side of the city where someone else can be disturbed. The people have spoken."

With that, Mrs. Gudrun cocked her chin in the air and pivoted 180 degrees. Her escorts each shot Alderman Sheedy a death glare before similarly pivoting to show their backs and the three slunk off like pouting jungle cats deprived of their meal.

"God. Damn. NIMBY's," Alderman Sheedy muttered under his breath.

It Takes a Village to Raise Property Values

❦

"This curse is inflaming a very touchy political situation."

Alderman Sheedy sat in his office with Mister Lewis. He'd broken out in a sweat after his close encounter of the geriatric kind and it had only grown worse.

"There's been a lot of fighting over that baseball stadium, even before the curse made things crazier. The owners are doing a lot of construction on the place. Lots of redevelopment. If they didn't get the permits, it's like Mrs. Gudrun said. They were going to move to the suburbs and start from scratch where the land was cheaper."

"That's not exactly unusual in this day and age," commented Mister Lewis.

"It's not that complicated," Alderman Sheedy attempted to explain. "The city's running a budget deficit. We get an amusement tax on every ticket to a game. We get a beer tax on every beer sold. We've got a food tax on every hot dog and peanut. We get the same tax in every bar that's sprung up around the neighborhood. We used to make a mint off parking tickets until that idiot mayor sold the city's parking concession, but we can still issue traffic tickets galore. All the better if they're tickets to suburbanites. We're going to build a new hotel. More tax from outsiders. We just can't leave all that tax money on the table while the city's in the hole.

"More importantly, I own a lot of property around here and development keeps my property value up and the rent I can charge up. I'm paying you because I'm not going to lose property value over a curse and I'm not losing the next election over it, either."

"So the primary goal is more about alleviating the political situation than dispelling any curse," asked Mister Lewis.

"That's... complicated," Alderman Sheedy rubbed his temples, the copious sweat substituting for massage oil. "There's a couple things going on. Mrs. Gudrun – the lady that was yelling at me about the bodies? She's in charge of the Ice Year Neighborhood Partners. It's a sort of neighborhood association. The worst Not In My Back Yard group you've ever seen. You think it's bad when somebody moves next door to a bar and complains there's a bar next door? That ballpark's well over a hundred years old and they act like it's new to the neighborhood.

"The thing is, they're senior citizens and they're the most regular voters there are. And more people listen to them than you'd think. They're taking advantage of curse breaking free of the stadium for another push to get rid of the ballpark. That can't happen and I don't want them coming after me if it doesn't."

"Then let's back up a little," suggested Mister Lewis. "Explain to me what you mean by the curse breaking free of the stadium."

"Right," said Alderman Sheedy. "So ever since the curse was placed on the stadium back in the forties, nothing ever goes right for the team. Either the team's terrible or something incredibly stupid happens to them before they can get to the World Series. They lose a game because a ball rolls between the outfielder's legs – straight out of a Three Stooges movie – or a fan interferes with a home run ball. That was the curse. No matter what, they just can't make it to the Series.

"So this year, it actually looks like their year. Since, you know, they're wanting to expand the ballpark and teams always seem to come back when it's time for construction. But this time it really looks like their year. More people are showing interest in the team than ever before. More money is being spent in the neighborhood than ever before. And the curse is so mad at all this, it's left the ballpark and is getting revenge on the fans."

"I don't think curses can get mad," Mister Lewis sighed. "The manifestation of the curse... it was like what we just saw? The goat avatars over their heads and effectively suicidal actions?"

"Those were the first direct deaths," replied Alderman Sheedy. "It started slowly. More drunk and disorderly behavior. More public urination and throwing up. Maybe a few more fights with visiting fans. Nothing that unusual, just a little more of it. And it's not like we want to discourage spending money around here. That's all part of the experience.

"So eventually we notice it's a little rowdier this year. After all, the team's winning for a change. So we put a few more cops on duty. And when we did that instead of showing the curse respect, that's when the goats started showing up. The same kind of behavior, but worse. A lot more volume when they toss their cookies on the street. A brawl instead of just shoving. Buzzkill on top of damages. And that's let the Ice Year Neighborhood Partners get some traction with evicting the ballpark."

"She called you cousin, is there family business involved," asked Mister Lewis.

"No," groaned Alderman Sheedy. "She calls all the public servants 'little cousin.' She seems to think we owe her something. Those NIMBY's are just weird and entitled. You need to take away what they can complain about."

"So, in theory, it would also be acceptable to push this curse back into the ballpark. Assuming that it's experiencing some sort of scope creep associated with the team's performance."

"I suppose," Alderman Sheedy wrinkled his brow. "As long as nobody dies inside the ballpark, I really don't care. Somebody dying during a game would be bad for business. And as long as those goat heads stop appearing, nobody's going to think a certain amount of bad behavior is out of the ordinary. But the Santa Stagger is next week…"

"You can't mean..." horror crept its way onto the face of Mister Lewis.

"That's right. 2,000 overgrown frat brats in Santa costumes blind drunk before they go on a 17 bar pub crawl. It's the worst weekend of the year. All by itself, Santa Stagger is worse than the curse. If the curse seizes on to it... it could be the Great Fire all over again. And that's not the worse part."

"How do you figure that?"

"As alderman, I get to be an agent of record for the Ward's insurance policies. We have that kind of a full scale riot, there's going to be claims. It'll blow my loss ratio and I won't get my low losses bonus. I will not have a 70-year-old curse costing me money!"

Well Behaved Guests

❧

"If you're right and this is a Greek curse we're dealing with," Mister Lewis spoke as he and the Alderman circled around the ballpark heading towards the largest concentration of bars in its shadow. "Then this is most likely some form of vaskania. It's more generically referred to as an 'Evil Eye.' If this is what's going on, that's simple enough to dispel."

"So it will be over tonight," pleaded Alderman Sheedy.

"If it's what you think it is," replied Mister Lewis. "The Evil Eye can be spawned through envy and rage. That's somewhat consistent with how you think the curse started. The rest of it, though... it's just not consistent. Could the gravitas of public attention running counter to the curse's goal be causing it to evolve in unusual ways? I don't know. We need a test subject. If you'd briefed me before I arrived, I could have tried exorcising any Eye from those lawn irrigators and perhaps they wouldn't have jumped in front of that truck."

The alderman did not reply and the two continued their way around the stadium. When they reached the opposite corner of the block, the strip of bars the next block over was starting to percolate and a small crowd was staggering from saloon to saloon with intent. They crossed the block and entered into the buzzed throng.

"How frequently does this occur," asked Mister Lewis.

"Too frequently," said Alderman Sheedy. "But we'll know pretty fast. None of this is subtle."

So they kept moving. The afternoon was fading, but the crowd wasn't. Twice around the block and by then, everyone was looking towards the northern sky. It started with a noise. An impossibly deep voice screaming "meh" boomed out of the sky with the last syllable trailing off in a jagged trilling. Then came a point of light, growing larger as it grew nearer until it turned into two shimmering goats pulling a chariot.

"Um, that's a new one," muttered Alderman Sheedy.

When the chariot was practically overhead, the reins attaching the goats to the chariot fell off and the goats shot into the crowd like they were arrows fired from a bow. When they hit the crowd, the goats disappeared.

A few seconds later there was a scream. The sort of bellowing you might expect to hear from a warrior charging into battle. The crowd parted a bit as a chair flew through the air, revealing a man with the build of an out of shape linebacker swinging fists at anything around him. Where his head should have been was the flickering visage of a goat.

Shortly after that, the scene repeated itself further down the block. A slightly more fit man with a flickering goat for a head was picking people up and tossing them.

"It always has to be hard way," Mister Lewis grumbled as he stomped over to the first goat headed man. He stared into the goat's eyes, raised his arms and spoke.

"Ο Κύριος ο Θεός μας, ο βασιλιάς των ηλικιών, παντοδύναμος και ισχυρό, που δημιουργούν και να αλλάξει τα πάντα με τη θέλησή σας και μόνο? που άλλαξε σε δροσιά τις φλόγες του φούρνου στη Βαβυλώνα, που είχε θερμανθεί επτά φορές περισσότερο από το συνηθισμένο, και διατηρούνται με ασφάλεια τα τρία ιερά νέους σας? η γιατρός και θεραπευτής των ψυχών μας? η ασφάλεια εκείνων που ελπίζουν σε σένα? σας προσευχηθούν και να παρακαλώ σας: Αφαιρέστε, το αυτοκίνητο και να εξορίσει κάθε διαβολική δραστηριότητα, κάθε σατανική επίθεση και κάθε οικόπεδο, το κακό περιέργεια και τη ζημία, και το κακό μάτι πονηρά και πονηρών ανθρώπων από τον υπηρέτη σου? και αν προκλήθηκε από την ομορφιά ή την ανδρεία, ή ευτυχία, ή ζήλια και φθόνο, ή το κακό μάτι, το κάνετε μόνοι σας, Ο Λόρδος που αγαπούν την ανθρωπότητα, απλώσει κραταιό χέρι σας και ισχυρό και ευγενή χέρι σας, να κοιτάξει κάτω από αυτό πλάσμα σας και να παρακολουθήσετε πάνω του, και να τον στείλει έναν άγγελο ειρήνης, μια πανίσχυρη φύλακας της ψυχής και του σώματος, που θα επιπλήξει και εξορίσει από τον κάθε πονηρό σκοπό, κάθε ξόρκι και το κακό μάτι των καταστροφικών και ζηλιάρης άνδρες? έτσι ώστε, φρουρείται από σας, ικέτης σας μπορεί να σας τραγουδήσω με ευχαριστία: Ο Κύριος είναι βοηθός μου, και δεν θα πρέπει να φοβόμαστε; τι μπορεί να κάνει ο άνθρωπος για μένα; Και πάλι: Θα φοβόμαστε κανένα κακό, γιατί είσαι μαζί μου."

The goat head tilted. A look something like puzzlement flashing across its eyes. Then its teeth gnashed and it lumbered towards Mister Lewis.

"It's not a Greek curse," Mister Lewis frowned as he spoke to Alderman Sheedy. "Fortunately, I have an equalizer. You might want to back up."

As the goat-headed man charged him, Mister Lewis brought his knee up into its groin. The eyes of the goat rolled back and it howled. Then separation occurred. The goat head blinked and shot back into the sky towards the chariot, which still floated above. A goat appeared in front of the floating chariot, once more tethered to it by a rein. The head of the man whose body the goat had been riding was now visible again, collapsed to the ground.

"Why, brah, why," the man groaned as his writhed on the sidewalk.

Mister Lewis repeated the process on the second man with a goat head. The same results followed. When the second goat appeared in the sky, attached by reins to the chariot, the goats began to start moving. The chariot turned in a circle behind the goats and they flew away in the direction they came from. Strangely, the second goat appeared to be walking with a limp.

"Did you magic them," squeaked Alderman Sheedy, clinging closely to Mister Lewis.

"No, the prayer against the Evil Eye didn't even register," said Mister Lewis. "On the other hand, nobody likes getting kicked in the balls. It doesn't work if an entity has settled in, but it's a helluva shock to the system if they haven't. We're not dealing with a Greek curse, though. And what I just saw cannot possibly exist."

"Whatever it was, we can't have berserkers tearing up the entertainment district," Alderman Sheedy was close to hyperventilating.

"Berserkers," mused Mister Lewis. "Yes. That would fit with the chariot. Except they're all long dead."

Alderman Sheedy opened his mouth to ask a question, but the words never made it out.

"More disturbances, little cousin," Mrs. Gudrun and her flankers had returned. "This all has to go. Shut down these ale halls. Banish the stick ball. These masterless thralls will tear each other apart and riot if things stay unchecked."

"Masterless thralls," stammered Alderman Sheedy, clearly confused.

"Slaves without masters," answered Mrs. Gudrun. "They do not own their land. They are like slaves to their wages and choose our neighborhood for their disruptions. It will only get worse. End this now, little cousin."

And once more, she turned and left. But this time her flankers' death glare fell on Mister Lewis, not Alderman Sheedy.

"Thralls," repeated Mister Lewis. "That's not a good sign."

"No respect for rental," Alderman Lewis had a rant bubbling up. "They don't like people who rent. Well, I rent out plenty of apartments and I don't need fear mongering driving down the price of rent. Just because Ice Year owns their condos..."

"Ice Year?"

"Yes, Ice Year Neighborhood Partners. It's the name of their association."

"I think it's supposed to be pronounced Aesir," Mister Lewis raised an eyebrow. "How can a Viking cult call down magic when their gods are dead?"

Consistently Inconsistent

ᏯᎦᏯ

Two hours later, Mister Lewis returned to Alderman Sheedy's office.

"Put this on your wrist," said Mister Lewis as he handed the Alderman a rope bracelet with a very worn metal charm shaped vaguely like a hammer hanging from it.

"What is it?"

"Thor's hammer," replied Mister Lewis. "Or at least an amulet that represents the protection of Thor and his hammer. At one time, it definitely would have been protection against Thor's wrath."

"At one time?"

"Yes. There's a lot that's not right here and that's part of it. The chariot and goats? That's consistent with Thor's chariot. The goats are named Tanngrisnir and Tanngnjóstr. That translates roughly to 'teeth-barer' and 'teeth grinder.' One of those goats had a limp, which is something the god Loki caused to happen to annoy Thor, but that's another story.

"Then you've the possessed people acting like berserkers while a war god's pets are on them."

"I thought Thor was the god of thunder," interrupted Alderman Sheedy.

"He was," answered Mister Lewis. "But he's an Aesir, and all the Aesir were war gods, first and foremost. Which brings us back to your friend Mrs. Gudrun. Her 'Ice Year' club is pronounced almost identically and she's going on about thralls. Thralls are what the Vikings called their slaves. If it weren't for all this business about a Greek curse, I'd almost say she was throwing it in your face."

"Why would Vikings hate baseball," asked Alderman Sheedy.

"A better question is how," said Mister Lewis. "The Viking gods are dead. Thor is dead. Ragnarok – the twilight of the gods – was real. It happened centuries ago."

"You mean like the Thor movies?"

"Well, sort of. But without all the Star Wars influences, lasers and spaceships. There weren't any dark elves invading, it was Loki betraying the Aesir to the giants. Loki's father was a giant and he ultimately took his father's side. The two sides wiped each other out. It was a real bloodbath. But there's no Thor for them to call on."

"Is it... Thor's ghost?"

"I'd like to say that's not possible, but very little of what we've seen makes any sense. Magic is not random. Now put on your amulet. You're going to go visit your Mrs. Gudrun, away from the prying ears of the public and accessible collateral damage. We'll try and figure out what exactly is happening here and if we're lucky, the amulet will work."

Chopping the Family Tree

❧

"Little cousin," Mrs. Gudrun, smiled for a change as she opened the door. "You've finally come for a family chat. Do come in."

Alderman Sheedy and Mister Lewis entered as they were bid to. They were ushered through the hallway into a massive and ornate parlor room with a twelve-foot ceiling. The place was furnished in what looked like 19th century furniture. Furniture that was expensive when it was made, but much more expensive now. The Ice Year Neighborhood Partners were well-heeled, indeed.

"Is this man your thrall," Mrs. Gudrun gestured to Mister Lewis.

"I am a free man," Mister Lewis had a slight edge to his voice.

"That's not really necessary," Alderman Sheedy attempted to interject but was cut off.

"We will conduct family business in the traditional

way," Mrs. Gudrun said not unlike a disappointed school teacher. "A jarl should present his men for introduction and present them for what they are. How much has the blood thinned in you? Now, little 'free man,' do you own property or just work for your jarl?"

"It's all in order, my chieftain," Mister Lewis put a bit of emphasis on "chieftain" and shot Alderman Sheedy a look to play along. "I own property elsewhere. I serve at Jarl Sheedy's pleasure."

"Very well," said Mrs. Gudrun as she turned to address Alderman Sheedy. "We have grown tired of your delaying tactics. They were old when your great grandfather used them and they have not aged well. That stick ball stadium grows more annoying by the day. These children that swarm around it cannot hold their liquor or their fluids. The noise they make. The very sight of them. We have had our fill and we will tolerate them no more."

"Now look," Alderman Sheedy finally had a topic where he thought he might have a leg to stand on. "That team stands a good chance of going all the way this year. That's good for business and you're going to have to get used to that."

"That team is going nowhere," Mrs. Gudrun's tone dropped an octave. "How many times in the last century have we seen to it they went nowhere in the most soul crushing way possible? I can't fathom why these fools keep coming back. They are not wanted here."

"They have to spend their money somewhere," the sweat was starting to bead up on Alderman Sheedy's temple again. "Better they spend it in my Ward. Things will stay as they are."

Alderman Sheedy swallowed hard and watched as Mrs. Gudrun's face became flush and her breathing deepened.

"Putting yourself above family, little cousin," hissed Mrs. Gudrun. "Perhaps you need reminding where your blood comes from."

Her posture straightened. The color of her hair darkened from white to a deep orangish-red and it started growing like a bramble bush. The rest of her was growing, too. In a few seconds, she was eight feet tall with long, pointy fingers and an even more disproportionally long nose.

"Your blood is weak," Mrs. Gudrun whispered into Alderman Sheedy's ear. "But not all of your blood is mortal. You would do well to remember your family or shall we find another little cousin to replace you as jarl of this Ward?"

She gestured behind her and where her usual flanking companions of elderly men stood, now towered two giants standing ten feet tall, wearing Nordic armor and looking strangely like Idris Elba. The giants took two steps forward.

Alderman Sheedy let out a whimper and reflexively threw his arms in front of his face, causing the amulet of Thor to pop out of his sleeve and dangle in front of him. The giants stopped and stared.

"You're wearing... the hammer of... Thor," Mrs. Gudrun stammered.

"You can't touch me," shouted Alderman Sheedy, peeking out between his arms.

"We need to leave," said Mister Lewis as he grabbed Alderman Sheedy by the back of his collar.

"You idiots," Mrs. Gudrun broke out laughing. "Thor has been dead for ages. He holds no power in this realm. You really don't know who your family is or you'd realize how sacrilegious it is to wear that thing. Halvard – ride his servant."

One of the Idris Elba lookalike giants was consumed by a glowing light, which shrank and settled into the form of a goat, just like from the chariot before. The goat flew through the air at Mister Lewis, but instead of a goat's head replacing his, the goat bounced off and the giant reappeared sprawled on the floor.

"Doesn't work on my kind," muttered Mister Lewis. "Time to go, Alderman."

"Oh little cousin," Mrs. Gudrun looked sad. "You hired a man to practice magic for you? A man? I will never understand this age. Some things are just not right. Give the 'free man' physical restraints."

Another gigantic Idris Elba ducked its head and entered through the parlor door, blocking the exit. He picked Mister Lewis up with two hands, while Alderman Sheedy fell over and curled up into a ball.

"Ground the magician with iron," ordered Mrs. Gudrun.

Mister Lewis was shoved into a high-backed chair and an iron pipe was bent around his chest and the back of the chair, effectively binding him in place.

"A history lesson little cousin," Mrs. Gudrun leant

over the whimpering form of Alderman Sheedy. "Lightning has always struck the leaves and brought fire. In doing so it brought our father and your great-great-grandfather. Nearly 150 years ago our father, lord of wildfire, let the lightning strike the leaves in this tired city. As it burned, he sowed his seeds widely. We are of the first generation. We settled here and we stayed. Why do you think this city's jarls are so close? Why do you think your elections hand down titles from father to son? You are of the wildfire, little cousin. The fifth generation of the divine ruling class."

"But, but," Alderman Sheedy struggled to form words. "Thor brings the lightning and you said he was dead."

"Are you an apostate as well," Mrs. Gudrun slapped him.

"The lightning," Mister Lewis spoke quietly. "Was from the giant Fárbauti of the Jötunn. The leaves were Laufey of the wooded isle. When the lightning struck the leaves, Loki was born. But Loki died with Thor during Ragnarök."

"What do your eyes see," asked Mrs. Gudrun.

"Giants who change their form."

"And your eyes do not lie," said Mrs. Gudrun. "Not unless we want them to. Were you expecting Loki's children to be wolves and serpents? We were all born to human mothers, not giantesses."

"I wasn't expecting Loki's children to be wearing the form of Idris Elba," replied Mister Lewis.

"Stringer Bell was a role model until his betrayal," retorted Mrs. Gudrun. "And there is virtue to be found in the act of betrayal. Not all entertainments are frivolous."

"Idris Elba is a king among peasants," said his outsized lookalikes in unison.

"Now hold on a minute," Alderman Sheedy was beginning to catch up with the situation. "You mean to tell me you were all living here before the stadium was built?"

"Since 1879," said Mrs. Gudrun. "Are you finally waking up to reality? We want our peace and quiet back."

"Oh my god," shrieked Alderman Sheedy. "You really are NIMBYs from hell!"

"Technically," said Mrs. Gudrun. "Hel is our sister and we don't plan on visiting her. You, however, might be visiting her soon if you don't start living up to the accommodations your side of the family pledged and you have conveniently forgotten about."

"If I'm a giant," Alderman Sheedy ventured a question. "Why can't I turn into somebody else like they can? Are you holding out on me?"

"This just isn't going to work," Mrs. Gudrun sighed. "I'll have some children of my own and arrange for them to be elected jarl or alderman or whatever they're calling it these days."

Mrs. Gudrun's form shrank and her features melted into those of Alderman Sheedy.

"You're very replaceable, little cousin," her voice was now the same as the Alderman.

She snapped her fingers and the giant she'd addressed as Halvard also morphed into a doppelganger of Alderman Sheedy.

"This is what will happen. Next weekend, your cousins will visit the Santa Stagger, much as they visited the ale houses today, but without your little magician to coddle the drunks. There will be a glorious battle. There will be blood. There will be death. And then I will appear in your form and start the overdue process of evicting that ridiculous stick ball team.

"Halvard and I will take turns playing your part until my own children are ready. Their blood will not be as diluted as yours. It should only take eight years or so before they're sufficiently grown to replace the likes of you. But for now, I think I'll eat you. I suspect I'll only taste mortal. Does anyone care for a wager?"

The Alderman Sheedy that used to be Mrs. Gudrun opened her mouth wide... and kept opening it. When her mouth was a gaping hole with a two foot radius, her teeth extruded into sharp points. Then she stepped forward towards the original Alderman Sheedy, who was frozen in shock on the floor, saliva dripping as she moved forward.

"Adjudication," hissed Mister Lewis.

"What," the Alderman Sheedy that used to be Mrs. Gudrun retracted her mouth and turned.

"This is a family dispute. On behalf of my client, I demand adjudication by the head of the family. It is the custom."

"I am the head of the family in this city," said the Alderman Sheedy that used to be Mrs. Gudrun. "This is my adjudication. I shall give you yours when I'm done eating."

"You are not the family's eldest," said Mister Lewis. "I

demand adjudication from the true head of the family. It is his right."

The Alderman Sheedy that used to be Mrs. Gudrun paused for a moment and then reverted to her guise as an elderly woman.

"Very well. We shall summon Father."

Father Knows Death

Lightning flashed, which was a little strange to be happening inside a house. Where the lightning had struck the floor, a circle of fire burned. Inside that circle of fire was a giant. A much larger giant than the ones already in the parlor, his shoulders were hunched as he leaned over to avoid putting his head through the ceiling. That head was topped with flowing red hair. An unusually thick red beard covered most of his face and dropped to mid-chest. Red and yellow flames danced where his eyebrows should be and matched twinkle in his eyes. He wore a massive fur coat, skinny jeans, yellow hi-top sneakers and a plain white t-shirt with "I Am Not A Hipster" written across it in bold black letters. Loki, the last of the Norse Gods, was exactly what his t-shirt said he wasn't.

"Hello children," said Loki. "Why I don't I make myself more comfortable?"

He shrank down to seven feet and took off his coat.

"That's better," he continued. "Now, did you have some mayhem in mind? It's been a very slow week and hearing some shrieks would be such a relief."

"My little cousin's magician demanded adjudication, father," Mrs. Gudrun nodded her head toward Mister Lewis. "My little cousin has forgotten his family duties."

"Technically, he's your nephew," said Loki. He ignored Alderman Sheedy and approached Mister Lewis, still bound to a chair with an iron bar. "Hello. I'm Loki. God of wildfire. God of tricksters. God of so very many things. How is it you come to speak for one of my children?"

"I thought Heimdall gutted you at Bifrost during Ragnarok," said Mister Lewis. "How is it you're still here?"

"He did," replied Loki. "And it hurt. But giants are very hard to kill. An expert like you should know that."

Loki paused, noticing some of the giants still wearing the form of Idris Elba.

"Why do you appear to me as Heimdall from that ridiculous Thor movie," Loki growled. "That's very disrespectful. I prefer to remember the burning of Asgard, not the pain in my gut."

"Idris Elba's been in other movies," muttered one of the giants, shifting back to his natural giant form.

"Now, where were we," continued Loki. "Oh, yes. How is it you come to speak for one of my children?"

"I don't think he's in any condition to speak for himself right now," said Mister Lewis, glancing at Alderman Sheedy sitting slack jawed on the floor. "I was retained to help him with the curse of the goat, but I can see this is a family squabble and I appeal to you in your role as god of self-interest."

"You say self-interest as though it were a bad thing," Loki wore a mock frown. "But what is family for if not self-interest? Pray continue."

"Your... other children have been threatening my client's livelihood and the value of his property. They wish to remove the baseball stadium from the neighborhood, which will cause..."

"Oh, that curse of the goat," interrupted Loki. "These mortal fools actually believed that? Oh, I love this town. They're so gullible. Curse of the goat... I just like getting their hopes up and dashing them. You did know I'm also the god of schadenfreude, didn't you?"

"He broke his covenant," interrupted Mrs. Gudrun. "When you sired the political class, it was agreed when their descendants inherited their offices that the first generations' wishes be attended to. The blood grows thin. This wretch is not the first offender, but he is the worst."

"You have a point," admitted Loki. "The blood is running a bit thin these days. I've never seen so many of my children getting arrested. I mean if you can't con a crowd that thinks a goat is keeping their team from winning, who can you con? They'll pretty much believe anything."

"We did not want that wretched stadium in the first place," Mrs. Gudrun ranted on. "The crowds have somehow managed to get more obnoxious and they're threatening to have another World Series. We could crush them again, but it's time to just remove the root of the problem. Send the team to the suburbs. The little cousin frets about taxes and his property value. I don't think quieting the neighborhood will do anything but enhance the price. We need more like minds, not blackout drunks."

"Now hold on a minute," Loki arched a flaming eyebrow. "Maybe you were trying to quiet the neighborhood, but I was sabotaging the team to mess with the fans. It's hard to cause so much distress with one act. Something like the ball rolling between the outfielder's legs doesn't just crush their own fans, it brings the ridicule of all the other cities. It's almost perfect. The only other thing that's come close was selling the parking ticket operation to one of my shell companies. Every time I raise rates I can hear a scream that's more tormented than the last."

Loki was also the god of assholes.

"You can bedevil them out in the suburbs," sighed Mrs. Gudrun. "We are trying to stick to the terms of our original agreement. I swear, Father, sometimes I forget you're older than me. May I please now eat this thin-blooded failure of a cousin?"

"I suppose," said Loki. "I don't think it will be nearly as much fun with boring suburbanites. Maybe I can get one of the players to marry a swinger again. That seems more suburban and the fistfights in the dugout are always amusing, plus it takes them forever to rebuild."

"You need to stop letting her undermine your authority," interjected Mister Lewis. "You really don't know what she's been up to in the name of Thor."

"Explain," the flames of Loki's eyebrows thickened as he squinted.

"She's been making public displays of magic using the trappings of Thor," said Mister Lewis. "It's one thing to use the image of goat around that stadium to scare off tourists. It's an entirely another to have Tanngrisnir and Tanngnjóstr appear in the sky above the stadium pulling a chariot. That's a good way to get Thor some new worshipers."

"Daughter," said Loki. "We've talked about public displays of magic. Not cool. Pumping up my dearly departed 'brother?' Also not cool. Bad enough he's got movies. Weird things happen when people start to believe and I don't need to deal with that."

"Oh, please," grunted Mrs. Gudrun. "Like anyone will believe that collection of drunks saw a phantom goat. Strictly a scare tactic to thin the herd."

"It seems like my client is the only one interested in preserving the way you want things run," said Mister Lewis.

Alderman Sheedy sat up and nodded his head.

"So many of my children wanting to preserve something," said Loki. "I think my children got old and settled into the banality of centuries past. Where is the fun in turning in early? When did they forget the joy of watching a train wreck? And let's be clear, your precious neighborhood has the best social train wrecks on Friday night.

"Still, it's just apples and oranges," Loki shrugged his shoulders. "We're going to have to have a talk about public displays of magic, but that's all because somebody didn't keep his end of a covenant. And I guess somebody's going to find out if he tastes good with ketchup. Rules is rules."

"And I suppose it's also OK with you, she's decided

the blood's too thin and is planning to repopulate the herd with children of her own," asked Mister Lewis.

Loki paused for a moment, then he turned and stared intently at Mrs. Gudrun. He frowned and shook his head.

"But that's okay," said Mister Lewis. "She's just trying to be like her old man. Oh, maybe it was an adopted family, but her old man still decided they were in his way and burned them down. It's probably just in the blood. Her blood is thicker than my client's, correct?"

"Point," said Loki.

For two minutes Loki said nothing. He just stared at Mrs. Gudrun.

"Can't have it," Loki finally said.

He snapped his fingers and a flame erupted from the floor and enveloped Mrs. Gudrun. She burned quickly and as her ashes fell, he swept his arm toward the next giant as though he was asking for the next dance. The flame danced to the next giant and then to the next until the parlor was strewn with ash and scattered flames. It only took a few minutes.

When it was over, Loki turned back to Mister Lewis.

"You earned your money," Loki said. "That was not fun. Necessary, but not fun. Your client owes you a bonus. Do you get bonuses in your line of work, magician?"

"Sometimes," replied Mister Lewis.

"Let's get a better look at you child," Loki grabbed Alderman Sheedy by the chin and gazed into his eyes. "Remind me, who was your daddy?"

"Horace Sheedy," squeaked Alderman Sheedy.

"Horace was one of mine," said Loki. "Great, great grandson. Or was that great, great, great? It doesn't really matter. I started the Sheedy's... the divine Sheedy's, that is... shortly after I started the Great Fire and burnt down half the city. Fires are a lot of fun. Great cover if you need to explain people disappearing and new ones arriving. Records get lost. People get distracted. And the chaos is good for the soul.

"Here's the thing, though. My blood isn't mortal. I can see my blood in my children. It gets too thin, I have to look kinda hard, but I can still see it. Horace might have thought you were his son, but you're not. You're one hundred percent mortal. It's not so uncommon. Eyes wander, although I'd think one of my children would know what went on in his own house. Thin blood, I suppose. That does explain the... misunderstanding."

Loki stood up and snapped his fingers again. A circle of flame sprang up around Alderman Sheedy.

"On the other hand, it just wouldn't be right if you walked away," said Loki. "You not being blood and all."

The circle collapsed and Alderman Sheedy fell to ash.

"Don't look so glum," Loki said to Mister Lewis. "You saved your client from the clutches of my daughter. It's a bit beyond you to know who's my bloodline and who isn't. Not your responsibility unless... no, you're much too young to be his real father.

"Still you really did do me a service. I am the god of self-interest after all. Having my children growing ambitions after 150 years of proper servility simply won't do. Don't get me wrong. It's great they grew up to be like their old man, but I know better than to let that flower come to bloom."

Loki stood up and walked towards the door. Before exiting he turned back towards Mister Lewis.

"Since my not-grandson can't tip you out for superior service, I'll give you a tip for him. That chair is older than this house and if you fall backwards, it will break and you can at least walk around. I probably shouldn't leave anything behind but ash. Fire in the hole."

Fires shot up along the walls as Loki exited the parlor. Sure enough, Loki was right. Mister Lewis tipped the chair over backwards and when it hit the floor, it broke apart. The iron pipe was still holding the back of the chair to him, and the pipe was definitely warming up, but he could walk.

As he staggered to his feet, Loki stuck his head back into the doorway to the parlor.

"By the way, magician... my not grandson did pay you in advance, right?"

Loki's head disappeared, but his laughter didn't. Mister Lewis ran through the parlor door, but Loki had vanished. Spirited away in a much older sense of the phrase. Mister Lewis fled the building, which was burning up at an unnaturally quick pace. As he tried to wiggle the iron bar off himself, Mister Lewis finally processed Loki's last words. No, Alderman Sheedy had not paid him in advance. In fact, once he'd arrived, things had progressed too quickly for a retainer to be exchanged. With his client dead, Mister Lewis could only draw one conclusion: the god of assholes owed him money.

ALL THE DEAD
MUSICIANS

Two Clients and a Funeral

❧

There were ravens at the funeral. It wouldn't have been out of place if The King in Vermillion had been fronting a goth act. Alas, he had been the King in Vermillion, not the King in Black and his music was about love, not gloom. Well, the act of love, if perhaps not always the emotion. Nonetheless, ravens were making an uninvited appearance.

"You won't have heard about all the deaths," Morty Smalls hissed. "The media only gets wound up about the pop stars. Blues artists, jazz, classical – they don't care, but they're dying off too."

"It doesn't make sense," added Chris Parker. "They're dying too close together and then all the crows at the funerals. Always with the fucking crows."

"Ravens, not crows," said their companion in the black suit and sunglasses. "There's a significance to ravens if what you suspect is true."

Smalls and Parker were recording executives and

usually at each other's throats. Owning rival agencies will do that in many lines of work, but a bit more venom came with the territory for the music industry. As unnatural as their cooperating was, it seemed more real than the deaths plaguing them. Since the ball dropped at Times Square, at least two or three musicians of some renown in their format had dropped dead each week. The number was probably higher, but as Parker said, the smaller players don't always make the obituary section. Still, clients were dying and while the death of larger clients did mean a burst in sales and the royalties that followed, replacing acts as quickly as they were dying off was a problem and nothing about this apparent culling seemed natural. When Smalls and Parker finally compared notes and realized the birds weren't the other executive trying a publicity stunt, they decided to do the corporate thing and hire a consultant who specialized in these matters.

Musicians had run-ins with otherworldly problems all the time. Metal bands experimenting with rituals for their stage shows and summoning up new friends. The Blues turning out to be more literal than expected in matters of crossroads and curses. Authenticity causes problems for amateurs. And sex magic. What was it with drummers and sex magic?

Mister Lewis was someone who consulted on such matters. That probably wasn't his real name. Officially he called himself a "physics consultant," probably as a joke, but his profession didn't really fit with the Bureau of Labor Statistics. His payments went to a bank in Panama and nobody knew very much about him, save that he could fix "physics" problems more often than not and clean up after himself. Which was why Smalls and Parker had engaged him to attend the funeral and look into the surge in memorial specials.

"Yes, definitely ravens." Mister Lewis gestured towards a tree branch where a tightly packed row of ravens perched and seemed to stare at a particularly weathered 70-something man in a leather trench coat who wobbled a bit as he puffed on his cigarette. "Is that who I think it is?"

"Yeah, that's Ken Michaels," replied Parker. "Don't ask me what's in that cigarette, though. Hard to tell with him."

"Birds are staring at him like he's food," chuckled Smalls. "He's the only one I'm not worried about dying. If fifty years touring with Gathers No Moss haven't killed him, nothing will. He's chemically preserved."

As Smalls continued to snicker, a raven took flight, circled once and landed on Michaels' finger like it was in a Disney cartoon. In a Disney cartoon, the bird chirps sweetly and lovingly. This wasn't a Disney cartoon. The raven screeched as though in pain and immediately flew away in a straight line. Its friends on the branch stayed there, still seeming to stare.

"No, definitely not the carrion they're looking for," said Mister Lewis. "You have good reason to be suspicious. None of this smells right... and ravens do smell where their food is."

Wakes Are Good For Repeat Business

❧

S ome wakes are quiet. Some wakes go out of control. The King in Vermillion's wake was never supposed to be under control in the first place since the King took the old adage of "love thy neighbor" to heart in a literal way.

Bawdy was expected, but Jerry Bubbles, a teen idol from Canada who'd had neither the courtesy to disappear after puberty nor the lack of alibis to get deported, had a habit of getting bawdy with other people's dates and two fights had already started.

"Any way you can exorcise that douche back to Toronto?" growled Parker as she tried to wipe a green drink of indeterminable mixers off her suit where it splashed as it flew off an overturned table.

"He hasn't been in possession of his soul for a long time," Mister Lewis apologized. "You know there's very little to be done about the soulless ones until they've run their course. Keep anyone you care for out of their wake and hope they were poor negotiators for their contract."

Parker, Smalls and Mister Lewis picked their way through the crowd and flying glasses to the VIP section of the rented out club. Even at a VIP wake, Ken Michaels rated the formal VIP room. It was just as well since it meant not having to duck any more projectiles and the privacy of a booth was helpful for what was usually a delicate topic.

Michaels sat in a corner booth in the back of the room, velvet drapes three quarters shut, leaving him in deep shadows. Strangely, he was alone, save for a bottle and three lines of cocaine on the table.

"Hey, Ken," Smalls stuck his head between the curtains. "You don't mind if we join you? Misery and company and all?"

Michaels gestured towards the opposite side of the booth. "Just having some bourbon and blow. Seems like a good time for it. I didn't bring enough to share, though."

"That's OK," Smalls slid into the booth. "I know where to find my own. I think you know Chris Parker already and this is Mister Lewis. You hear about Otis Winslow's trip to the crossroads? Mister Lewis is the one who, um, navigated him back."

"Never really believed that happened," Michaels said as he pulled a silver cocktail straw out of his coat and inhaled the first line. "People see a lot of strange things when they're fucked up."

"It's a strange world," Mister Lewis said, as he looked quizzically at the straw.

"It's an awful world," Michaels sucked up the second

line and sank deeper into the shadows. "Too many people dying and too many of them I know."

Michaels paused and leaned over the third line. Instead of coming out of deep shadow, the deep shadow leaned forward with him. He snorted. His eyes rolled back and Michaels convulsed once. As the convulsion ended, the deep shadows around him flickered and then seemed to flee the booth.

"I just don't feel this stuff like I used to," Michaels sighed as he blinked.

"Is it cold in here all of a sudden?" Smalls was sweating despite his complaint.

Any answers were cut off by screaming in the main room.

The VIP room cleared out quickly, as happens when the noise of a brawl ends with a scream. It was another dead musician. A drummer lay across a table, dead eyes staring at the ceiling and a trickle of blood leaking from his nose.

"I didn't touch him!" shouted Bubbles in a most un-Canadian tone. "But I'm going to touch his date. Where is she?"

A chair flew at him, but his charmed life continued and it missed him by a quarter of an inch.

"Everyone dying and that's what gets to live," muttered Michaels. "I can't believe it."

"That straw you use," Mister Lewis nodded to the hand Michaels still held it in. "Is it engraved?"

"Why yes, yes is it," Michaels beamed. "I can't figure out what it says, though. It was a gift from a fan in New Orleans. We played a New Year's Eve show down there this year. Or at least I think we played. New Year's Eve is usually a little fuzzy for me."

"It's very nice," said Mister Lewis. "Probably best we're all out of here before the ambulance arrives, though. Too many people getting asked too many questions."

Mister Lewis turned, grabbed Smalls and Parker by their elbows and hissed "Quickly and quietly out the front. The ravens aren't the only things hovering over Ken Michaels."

How Many Deities Does It Take To
Keep a Soul Screwed In?

❦

Parker's office wasn't the usual setting for a field briefing, but it was close and the agents were unsettled by what they saw.

"That shadow around Michaels," Smalls said slowly and quietly. "That wasn't really a shadow, was it?"

"No," Mister Lewis agreed. "That was almost certainly a manifestation of Death."

"I thought Death was supposed to be a lady," Smalls offered.

"I really wish you wouldn't fetishize a primal force like that," Mister Lewis shook his head.

"Hey, man – that's part of the music business," Smalls shrugged. "You know a better way to sell t-shirts?"

"Never mind that," interrupted Parker. "What really happened at the wake?"

"The what is easy, the why less so," began Mister Lewis. "When Ken Michaels snorted the third line he had a seizure. Normally when that happens, a person gets sick or dies. But Ken Michaels didn't die. I suspect he hasn't died on schedule for several months. Death was waiting and when Death was denied Ken Michaels, Death had a tantrum and took that drummer. Possibly a tantrum took the King in Vermillion. Possibly a tantrum took out some of your earlier clients. But there are definitely tantrums and Death is taking... I believe the economists would call it substitute goods. Other musicians."

"He couldn't have done this himself, could he?" Smalls asked.

"Ken Michaels is no sorcerer," Mister Lewis chuckled. "No, most likely he was enchanted by that fan he mentioned who gave him that silver straw. I need to get another look at it, but it's most likely a focal point for what's happened to him. Whoever gifted it is probably responsible for this."

"This isn't... the work of the Great Old Ones?" Smalls asked.

"Unlikely," Mister Lewis replied. "If the straw was given to him in New Orleans, it's more likely to be Voodoo at work. Unfortunately, he was probably blackout drunk for most of whatever happened there. I'd bet money he doesn't even realize anything's amiss.

"But I am going to need to take a closer look at that straw."

Drowning Other People's Sorrows

T he after party for the wake was in a club much like the first. The crowd was much the same, just a bit wobblier and worse for wear. Then again, the phrase "party like a rock star" didn't exist for no reason.

Once more Ken Michaels sat alone in a booth in the VIP room, this time the velvet was swapped out for a less tasteful gold lamé curtain. There was no drug paraphernalia on the table, just a bottle of shockingly cheap bourbon that the club still charged $150 for. Not to put too fine a point on it, but his right eye and left eye weren't looking in the same direction.

"You alright, Ken?" Smalls asked as he approached. "You look a little green."

"Green?!?" A confused Michaels muttered. "I must be drunk. I could've sworn this place was done up in gold."

Smalls and Parker exchanged what normally would

have been a knowing glance, but this time was more nervous than knowing.

"Could you tell them to put the lights back up?" Michaels swayed a bit in the booth. "These dimmers should be pre-show only."

The lights in the room weren't being dimmed, but the shadow was looming over Michaels again and as it thickened and lowered around his head, it might as well have dimmed his immediate area. Michaels leaned forward and took a labored breath and threw up a stream of dull red liquid across the table and all over the cushions on the opposite side of the booth. The shadow swirled about him and then shot away.

"He's bleeding out," stammered Parker.

"No," said Mister Lewis stepping towards the table. "That's not the right color. What were you mixing your bourbon with Ken?"

"What? Oh. That's probably the red wine I had in the limo. Did a couple shots of tequila, too. I'll be fine. I just need to get it out of..."

He threw up again, this time with a bit more arc on the stream.

"That's better. Makes room for more."

Michaels slid to the edge of the booth, pulled himself up, picked up the not quite empty bourbon bottle and moved one booth down.

"I find a claret refreshing in the afternoon. Maybe I should switch back. Does this place have claret?"

"Might be a better place for a Sazerac," offered Mister Lewis. "I got a taste for them in New Orleans."

"That's a good town," slurred Michaels, who slumped a bit in the booth. "Order them up."

"You said you had some special fans in New Orleans," probed Mister Lewis.

"Oh, there's a regular group," said Michaels. "Can't really call them a strange bunch, 'cause, you know... rock and roll, but they're out there. Creatures of habits with their little rituals, always with the big jewelry and symbols on the jewelry. Real friendly, though. They know what they like and... dammit, what is with the lights in this place?"

Death's shadow had returned.

"These fans," continued Mister Lewis, "were they locals?"

"Oh, it's a melting pot down there. Some native, some from Europe. Everyone likes the culture."

An electronica version of "Buttons and Bows" rang from a phone as everyone stopped and stared at Morty Smalls.

"I reimagine classics," growled Smalls before answering. He didn't stay on the phone long, though he was a half shade paler before he hung up. "Gheorghes Lamarr just died."

He was met with blank stares.

"Jazz flutist? Three Grammies? You people have no respect for culture."

"I don't suppose you topped off your nose while you were drinking," Mister Lewis asked Michaels.

"No, but that's a great idea."

Michaels produced a pouch and formed a line on the

table before pulling his silver straw out of his jacket. The shadow hanging over him pulsated slightly and Mister Lewis stared intently at the straw as Michaels drew the powder into his nose.

This time, the shadow stayed put.

Funeral Planning For Fun and Profit

❧

Back at Parker's office, the clients were hearing things they didn't want to hear.

"It's not as simple as that," Mister Lewis tried to explain. "Death is only taking a substitute life when Michaels would normally die, not just when he uses the straw. You saw the shadow linger when he took his last line. It's the difference between indulgence and over indulgence. What they used to call death by misadventure in old Hollywood."

"Oh, we get it," Parker was shaking her head. "But we know him. If somebody dies every time he'd normally overdose... that could be three times a day."

"Well, yes – it does explain why a fan would feel compelled to enchant him like that. Clearly, his endurance is already unusual, but nature has its limits."

"Nobody's arguing that," groaned Smalls. "And if he were my act, I might pay for the enchantment. I could see it earning out. But he's killing our businesses. Literally.

Love the player, hate the game, but this game has got to stop."

Mister Lewis stared at Smalls and Parker for a few seconds before responding.

"I have a good idea how this was done and it's not something that can simply be undone. It has to be contradicted. Put into conflict with another source of similar power and burnt out. And that's assuming it doesn't burn out the other source first, in which case you're back to square one with somebody asking questions about what happened to the curse they placed."

"So, you're saying you need to put him in a room with something Satanic," asked Smalls.

"It doesn't have to be Satanic, per se. It just has to be entering into conflict. Michaels has been enchanted to not die. It could be an entity that's actively attempting to cause him harm. Or his intended death could be an indirect result of what's set in play. You want the enchantments hitting each other and wearing each other out. Like grinding gears until they fall apart or stripping a screw."

"Then he has to die for this to end," asked Parker.

"There will have to be collateral damage," sighed Mister Lewis. "That's unavoidable. If the enchantment burns out at the right time, perhaps not, but Death will be looking to take someone. If it goes wrong, I may not be able to control the direction of that collateral damage. Or it might not work at all. Question: have either of you ever been musicians?"

After a burst of laughter, Parker was the first to regain composure.

"Mister Lewis, really. We're management. Nobody goes into management if they could get into a band."

"Then you're not likely to be who Death takes if this goes wrong. It's a business for me, too, and I need someone to invoice. That Satanic idea is not without merit. If someone sold their soul to be lucky and you drew that luck into conflict, it might be indirect enough to be relatively clean. If not, the damage might be acceptable. It will probably require... do either of you partake of cocaine?"

This time it was Smalls who finished laughing first.

"You really think musicians can afford to buy it themselves on their first contract? We're management."

Double Check That Contract

A nother day, another club and the wake's after party had merely switched locations. Such was the lifestyle. A slightly more coherent Ken Michaels sat in yet another VIP booth as Smalls, Parker and Mister Lewis approached him.

"I seem to be reaching the age where I get management visiting instead of groupies," quipped Michaels.

"Well, if you're looking for that..." began Mister Lewis, "perhaps you could introduce us to Jerry Bubbles?"

"That wanker? Oh, you won't want groupies after you meet him. All about master and servant with that one. You have to be really lucky to be that successful with no talent and that personality. Why don't you go fetch him, Chris? He'll take it better if you're my emissary."

Parker returned shortly with Bubbles in tow. Which is to say with Bubbles rubbing up against her and leering as if to say "you know you want it."

"I guess the party's starting," said Smalls, as he smirked at Parker. A tiny silver spoon appeared in his right hand and baggie in his left.

"Oh, that's too small for how I roll," screeched Bubbles. He jerked the end of a necklace from beneath his shirt, with a larger silver spoon dangling from the tip.

"Wankers. Bloody wankers and amateurs," mumbled Michaels as he displayed his silver straw.

"I need that," screamed a wide-eyed Bubbles.

"I don't think you're ready for a touch of class," Michaels said dismissively as he watched Smalls draw the lines with unseemly anticipation.

"I said I need that," Bubbles screamed as he grabbed for the silver straw.

As Bubbles and Michaels wrestled over the straw, the shadow formed over Michaels again. It swirled and vibrated, almost as if in excitement. Richards grimaced and moved his free hand to his heart as he younger Bubbles wrenched the straw free and positioned it over a line.

"Careful," interjected Mister Lewis. "That stuff will kill you."

"Not fucking likely," sneered Bubbles before he snorted.

As the powder hit his nostrils, the shadow leapt from Michaels to Bubbles... and then it paused, hovering. Flames flickered underneath the shadow as it started swirling around Bubbles. Bubbles swayed as though the shadow was kicking up a wind. His head snapped back and his eyelids parted to show flames where his eyes should have been.

The blazing eyes seemed to repel the shadow, which bounced back to swirl around Richards, now doubled over with both hands clutching his chest. But after one revolution, it bounced back to Bubbles. For twelve seconds, the shadow bounced from man to man, picking up a bit of flame around its edges each time it danced around Bubbles.

After twelve seconds, the shadow enveloped Bubbles. Then the flames and the shadow blinked out as though they were one and he face planted on the table.

"Did he just shit himself?" asked Smalls as a strong odor made itself known.

"No, that's brimstone," said Mister Lewis.

"Where is my client?" came a booming voice from across the room.

A slender man with abnormally large and piercing eyes glared at the booth as he approached it.

"I am Mr. Bubbles' agent," hissed the man. "What. Has. Transpired?"

"He borrowed the gentleman's straw," answered Mister Lewis. "I don't think it agreed with him."

The man glared at Mister Lewis, then at the straw, and then back to Mister Lewis.

"Ten years of luck used up in an afternoon?"

"He probably should have structured his contract differently," said Mister Lewis with a shrug of his shoulders.

"Structure is a more common problem than you might think," the slender man said with an edge in his voice. "However, his contract does seem to have expired. I'll see that he gets... home."

The man hoisted Bubbles onto his shoulder, turned and started walking away.

"What the hell was..." Smalls had turned to ask Mister Lewis, but a sound like a preternaturally loud crackling fireplace interrupted him.

When the party turned to see where the noise came from Bubbles and his agent was nowhere to be seen.

"Oh, that's not good," groaned a visibly pained Michaels.

"What's wrong?" asked Parker.

"The chest pain's gone, but it feels like a year's worth of hangovers picked now to come to visit," moaned Michaels. "It's OK, I feel worse for that wanker's agent."

Mister Lewis looked at the straw, lying where Bubbles had dropped it, glanced back to where Bubbles and agent were last seen, then back at Michaels. He exhaled.

"I suppose someone has to have sympathy for the devil."

LEGAL TERMINATION OF A WARLOCK

Employment Law

❦

"We need your help with a Warlock problem," said the woman from Human Resources. "But first, is 'Warlock' a term that's appropriate for a business setting? I really haven't had this kind of a problem before and I wouldn't want to be using inappropriate language."

"It's a matter of personal preference," replied Mister Lewis. "It would depend on your policy about gender specific terminology and the local history of its usage. The term can be a little touchy in Massachusetts, given the problems with persecution, but it's also a technical term. Your mileage may vary, as they say."

"Do you identify as a Warlock," asked the woman from Human Resources.

"A Warlock? That's not what it says on my business card."

Indeed, Mr. Lewis had a business card that said "Physics Consultant." It was something of an in-joke.

While Mr. Lewis did consult, he consulted on things that fell outside the laws of physics and sometimes went bump in the night.

"I... see," said the woman from Human Resources. "Well, I suppose Witches and Warlocks are not a protected class."

"Not necessarily," replied Mister Lewis. "Witches will still fall under gender protections and depending on the flavor of Witch or Warlock, there may be a basis for a religious discrimination suit. Legitimately."

"I hadn't thought about the religious implications," said the woman from Human Resources.

"You could always try to contest the validity of the religion, but then you get a media circus and when you're dealing with a Warlock, there's always the possibility his deity shows up feeling wrathful about being slighted. It's the sort of thing that's best to be avoided."

"Is everything I tell you strictly confidential?" asked the woman from Human Resources.

"Of course. I deal in discrete solutions."

"Given the nature of the software business, our CEO and founder really frowns upon having staff over the age of 30. This is a little bit of a grey area, but I understand that Warlocks are sometimes much older than they physically appear?"

Mister Lewis paused, took a deep breath and exhaled slowly before answering.

"I wasn't aware 30 was the mandatory retirement age in this country, but yes, sometimes a Warlock will be much older than he appears. Like the religious issue, it depends a bit on what kind of a Warlock he is."

"Good to know," said the woman from Human Resources. "I've been told to clear the decks of all employees over 30, so what I need your help with is identifying the Warlock and then documenting a separate case of actionable infractions so that we may successfully terminate his employment without concern for legal reprisals. The company comes first, so if we can't document anything actionable, we'll have to manufacture something once you've identified him."

"I suppose the first step," suggested Mister Lewis, "would be to determine if there's really a Warlock or it's just a case of assumptions being made."

"If he's not over 30, I'll have to ask management if they still want to terminate him. You can't age him if he's not over 30 can you?"

"Causing a body to age doesn't change the birthday," Mister Lewis suppressed a groan but wasn't able to stop his eyes from rolling.

Such a Friendly Office

❧

"It's probably easier for you to observe what's happening," said the woman from Human Resources as they left her office. "I'm sure I don't know your trade jargon."

"We can keep things to conversational English," replied Mister Lewis. "What specifically has been happening?"

"Keep three feet behind me and watch the floor as soon as we turn that corner. You'll get an eyeful."

They came to the end of the hall and turned the corner. The woman from Human Resources looked back at Mister Lewis, flashed a smile that wasn't smile, straightened her skirt and took a step forward. That's when the floor changed underneath her.

The color drained out of what had been a dull beige carpet and when the color left, a reflective surface replaced it. She stepped forward and the reflected area expanded forward with her. After four steps, a wolf whistle sounded seemingly from nowhere and the carpet faded back to beige.

"There isn't always a whistle," said the woman from Human Resources.

"How long does it normally follow you," asked Mister Lewis.

"It doesn't always. Sometimes it appears as a wide circle you just have to walk out of. Sometimes it blinks in and out every other step. Once I saw the reflection of Big Ben and the Eiffel Tower on either side of me."

"I see London, I see France," Mister Lewis smirked. "I'm going to go out on a limb here and guess this only happens when someone's wearing a skirt?"

"Yes. It's clearly harassment, but so far there hasn't been anyone to accuse. If it keeps up, the company will get sued regardless of who's doing what and..."

"HR's job is to protect the company," Mister Lewis finished the sentence. "So you think we're looking for a Warlock suffering from arrested development? Incidentally, has anyone worn a kilt in this office? It might be worth checking to see if gender is a spell trigger or just a type of garment."

"Not that I'm aware of. Now observe."

The woman from Human Resources reached into a cubicle and put a tentative hand on a chair. Slowly, she pulled the chair out into the aisle, keeping the back of the chair facing her. She then stepped in front of the chair, sat down and in an even and deliberate motion, swiveled the chair to face Mister Lewis. When the chair stopped moving, the sound of flatulence exploded forth. Again, she wore the smile that wasn't a smile.

"Every chair, or just that chair," asked Mister Lewis.

"Always this chair, but sometimes other chairs."

"Men or women affected?"

"Just women. Now let's go to the kitchen."

So they went to the kitchen. It was a fancy kitchen as far as office kitchens went. Three microwaves. An expresso machine. Marble counters. A kegerator. And a large stainless steel refrigerator whose door the woman from Human Resources was opening.

She produced a small cardboard box. The box was bright red with "Garden of Healthy Delights" stamped on it in foil.

"This is a box lunch," she said. "An expensive box lunch. Only the best for our employees. Open it up. You'll find a vegan chicken sandwich with lettuce and a slice of vegan provolone on a gluten-free bun."

Mister Lewis opened the box and examined the sandwich he found inside.

"I've never really understood the point of a gluten-free bun when vegan meat substitutes are made with wheat gluten."

"Just take a bite."

So Mister Lewis took a bite. He chewed twice and stopped.

"That's right," said the woman from Human Resources.

Mister Lewis spat the bite of sandwich into his left hand and poked at the remnants with the index finger of this right hand. Instead of lumps of wheat gluten, there had been actual chicken meat in his mouth.

He glanced back at the sandwich. No, that was definitely a meat substitute between the gluten-free buns.

"Carnivorous transmogrification," muttered Mister Lewis.

"If you took what you spit out to a lab, you'd find the bun wasn't gluten-free anymore, either."

"And this happens some of the time or all of the time?"

"All of the time. And the gluten-free buns always change to gluten. One of our programmers has Celiac disease. It's a problem and we've incurred liability if he wants to press the point."

"It definitely could be a Warlock," mused Mister Lewis. "The reflections and... noises... could easily be poltergeist activity, but transmogrification usually isn't."

"We didn't hire you for a poltergeist," the woman from Human Resources cut him off. "You can't fire a ghost. We're going to have a lawsuit on our hands, maybe several, if we don't fire somebody and blame this on them. Even if it were a ghost, I'd need to fire Charlie."

"You're that certain you know who's causing this?"

"Mr. Foster says Charlie is the culprit and has to go. Mr. Foster's word is law, so we're just here to arrange it."

The Alleged Warlock

Ｔhe alleged Warlock sat in his chair, typing away at his computer. He was an engineer. A coder of programs. For all the suspicions that this was an aged sorcerer, he sure didn't show the ravages of time. No, this alleged Warlock had the face of a fifteen-year-old boy. The kind of face where nobody believes his ID isn't a fake when he tries to get a drink. But isn't that what you'd expect someone to look like if they were clinging to youth by unnatural methods?

His attire didn't really match his face. A tweed sport coat with patches on the elbows over a plaid sweater vest over an Oxford shirt with a bright red bow tie. He dressed like a retired professor who spent his days in a private club alternating between snifters of brandy and naps.

Mister Lewis and the woman from Human Resources gazed at the alleged Warlock from over the cubical wall behind him.

"Mr. Foster is right," hissed the woman from Human

Resources. "No twentysomething coder would ever dress like that."

"Are you sure he's not just a hipster dressing ironically," asked Mister Lewis.

"No, coders wear hoodies. It's their uniform. I almost didn't hire Charlie because he didn't wear a hoodie."

"I didn't realize programming was a customer facing position."

"Of course not. But when there aren't enough programmers to go around, we encourage their herd mentality. If they assume that wearing the hoodie is their version of a suit and tie, it lets them feel special without cultivating actual individuality. As long as they think they're in uniform, it keeps them insecure and full of self-doubt. You don't need individuals on an assembly line and that's what large scale coding is. You need meek worker bees in hoodies with their heads down."

Mister Lewis watched the alleged Warlock typing away.

"He looks like he's a fast worker," whispered Mister Lewis. "Is he considered fast?"

"He's actually our fastest."

"Then I think it's time we were introduced."

The alleged Warlock was oblivious to their approach, in that peculiar mental place that is simultaneously zoned out and locked in on his work. Mister Lewis peered over the alleged Warlock's shoulder and noticed something odd. While the alleged Warlock's fingers were gliding over the keyboard, he wasn't actually pressing any keys. And even if he had been, the characters were appearing on the screen faster than he would have been typing.

"Everything good today Charlie," the woman from Human Resources said a little too loudly and a little too smarmily.

The alleged Warlock jumped a little as he looked up. Characters continued appearing on the screen for two seconds after his hand left the keyboard.

"Um, fine," squeaked the alleged Warlock. "To what do I owe the pleasure?"

"I'm just showing a visitor around the office."

She gestured towards Mister Lewis.

As she brought up her hand to make that gesture, it brushed against her skirt and the color started draining from the carpet. As the floor turned into a carpet textured mirror, Mister Lewis looked in the reflection of the alleged Warlock's face. He still looked like he was fifteen-years-old. A fifteen-year-old boy who was startled and not quite able to process what was being reflected beneath the woman from Human Resources, who coughed and quickly stepped back. The reflective surface did not follow her this time and faded away.

"Time for the rest of the tour," the woman from HR said, already walking away from the cubicle.

"You saw that," she growled when they were out of earshot.

"I saw three things, which one are you talking about?"

"That mirror under my skirt."

"Which seems to appear all over this office. Suspicious, but circumstantial at this point."

"Well, what about how fast he was typing?"

"There's something going on there, alright. It isn't necessarily related to your other problems, though. Surely you wouldn't fire somebody for being a fast programmer?"

"I'd fire him for being an ancient Warlock and polluting our corporate culture in a heartbeat."

"Yes, well, that's the sticking point. When that magic mirror popped up under you, I looked at his reflection in it and he still looked like a kid."

"Why would his magic not work in a mirror? We have lots of mirrors here."

"Yes, but when you look at an enchanted reflection, you normally see what's real, not an illusion. It means one of two things. Either he's really that young or he's very scary and we need to be cautious."

A CEO's Office Is His Castle

❧

"Mister Lewis, this is our CEO, John Foster," the woman from Human Resources said as she and Mister Lewis peered through the doorway of an office that looked more like a clubhouse. Three men were in the room, if men was the right word. It wasn't clear if any of them were old enough to have graduated from college. All wore dark grey hoodies with the logo of their company on them. Two sat in overstuffed chairs along the back wall, one holding the funnel end of a beer bong aloft for the other who was chugging away. The CEO was bent over his desk while holding an oversized silver goblet.

"Good to see you Toots," the CEO didn't bother looking up from the oversized book on his desk he was pouring over. "We can't seem to find a good title for our new hire in The Big Book of $tartup $ucess. Is Vice President of Hospitality a good title or is Chief Hospitality Officer better?"

"Is this for the waitress," the woman from Human Resources face didn't actually move when she spoke. It was that near omnipresent smile that wasn't really a smile and the words came through her teeth. Mister Lewis couldn't quite make up his mind if she wasn't the sincere sort or she hated her life.

"No, that would be boring," said the CEO. "She's the VIP hostess at the Modesty House nightclub. It's going to be great. We hire her half time and we'll get our drinks comp'd. Then we can take clients and investors there and we don't have to pay for entertainment expenses. And then she can hang around the office and greet people when they come in."

"I think that's called a receptionist," her voice continued to come through her teeth.

"No, no," said the CEO. "She won't be nearly appreciative enough while she's hanging out in the office if we don't give her a big title. I just want to make sure it's all by the book."

"He means The Big Book of $tarup $uccess," the woman from Human Resources, desperate to change the subject, turned to Mister Lewis. "It's this year's management fad. There's a new one every year. Six Sigma. Lean. As long as there's a numbered list of steps, preferably in a circle and you follow those steps to the letter, investment money will pour in and you're guaranteed a success. $tarup $uccess is the new new thing."

"Business needs to have immutable laws – like physics does," the CEO stood up. He wasn't as baby-faced as the alleged Warlock, but he'd still have trouble when he got carded. Perhaps hiring a hostess would cut down on questions of whether he was old enough to drink, too. "All we have to do is follow the book and give the investors what they want. Step one: book. Step three: money. But I can't find the right title for her in the book."

"We should focus on the matter of the firing," subject changed, she tried to steer the conversation back to what was originally intended. "Mister Lewis has met Charlie."

"Great," the CEO took a pull from his goblet. "How are we getting rid of the ancient bastard?"

"We haven't established that he's ancient... yet," replied Mister Lewis. "The concern about his age comes from that book?"

"Absolutely," the CEO also had a smile that lacked sincerity. "Chapter 3. 'And the great god Zuckerberg said "I want to stress the importance of being young and technical. Young people are just smarter." So shall be your hiring policy. Suffer not the aged employee, for he will negotiate and go home for supper.' All the investors agree. Younger is better. They loved me because I dropped out of Crocker University before I could even get a transcript. I have no baggage that keeps me from saying yes to the money."

"The great god Zuckerberg?"

"Absolutely. Startups are religion. It's a lot like the gospel of prosperity, really. Founders are to be worshiped and liquidation events are our eternal reward. The management book is our commandments. Some of the investors are even angels. Having aged workers violates a commandment and will be frowned upon by the investors. We need to keep the cash flowing and follow those commandments."

The woman from Human Resources cleared her throat.

"We also need to address the source of these mysterious mirrors and the kitchen problems and avoid litigation."

"I like the mirrors," slurred the hoodie-wearing bro on the receiving end of the beer bong.

"So do I," said the hoodie-wearing bro on the funnel side of the beer bong.

"It can't be helped. While Mister Lewis cannot confirm Charlie is older than he looks, he agrees with your suspicions about him."

"It takes a thief to catch a thief," said the CEO, his eyes narrowing a bit.

"Something like that." Mister Lewis frowned. "It could be he's the lightest touch typist I've ever seen, or else he's typing with his mind. It's inconclusive, in terms of the manifestations you're having trouble with. It might not be related, but it's suspicious and I'll be taking a closer look at him. That said, there are no indications that he's any older than he appears to be."

"He's probably got an old soul," the CEO said with a chill in his voice. "Investigate and shit. Make the investors happy. I'm the CEO. I really shouldn't need a reason if I want to fire someone. Failing fast isn't just about startups, it's about employees, too."

"But Mr. Foster," the woman from Human Resources interrupted. "Failing fast was from the previous management fad. We don't want to cause confusion by mixing fads."

"Perhaps there's something to be said for tradition," muttered the CEO. "Just get to it."

"I'll observe and report," said Mister Lewis.

"You do that," said the CEO. "And Toots, what title should we use with the new hire?"

"Vice President of Hospitality or Chief Hospitality Officer," asked the woman from Human Resources.

"That's right."

"If in doubt, we can spin it to the investors that we're creating an innovative new C-level position. The C.H.O."

"Yeah, I was leaning that way. But I don't think we should just call it by the initials. I think we should call it the C-HO. Makes her sound more... accommodating. And isn't that what hospitality is all about?"

The woman from Human Resources shuddered involuntarily as she left the room.

The Nice Doggie

T he alleged Warlock left work at 5 pm on the dot. It occurred to Mister Lewis that such a departure was in keeping with the management book his clients clung to so fiercely, should the alleged Warlock turn out to be an "aged employee."

The alleged Warlock either wasn't good at spotting a tail or was unaware that he should be looking for one. In an office where people seemed to have certain traits of either heightened focus or obsessive-compulsive disorder, it made the big picture a bit more ambiguous. Down the street, take a left, up three blocks, left another two and then he stopped in a park and planted on a bench.

A rendezvous or a habit? For five minutes, no one approached him and he sat with a faraway look on his face. People passed, still he sat, gazing into the distance. Ten minutes. Fifteen minutes. And then he was finally approached by a stray beagle.

Or was it a stray? The dog was borderline mangy, but it walked straight to him and was staring him square in the eye. Could it be the alleged Warlock had a Familiar?

The alleged Warlock stood up, patted his leg as though he wanted the dog to follow and walked towards the edge of the park. The dog did follow. Before he left the park, the alleged Warlock plucked two flowers from a bed. He walked north for a block and turned into an alley. The dog followed him.

By the time Mister Lewis had closed the block's distance he'd been following at, the alleged Warlock and the dog were deep in the alley. The alleged Warlock had placed the flowers on the ground and was twirling a silver chain roughly 20 inches long over the flowers. The flowers were melting into a liquid. After the liquid pooled, it rearranged itself into a not quite crescent shape and started to grow, like air being blown into plastic. It started to take on the texture of meat. Half of it turned red, half of it collapsed into shreds of a flower stem.

The dog pounced on the half that looked like meat and started chewing.

"You're new at transmogrification," said Mister Lewis. "I see you've got some talent transforming plants into meat, but increasing the volume during transmogrification is tricky. It works better when you're just changing a vegan sandwich to meat and it stays the same size."

"Do I know you," the no longer alleged Warlock's head spun around and he dropped his silver chain.

"We met at the office. And we need to talk about the

office. About the kitchen and the mirrors and the breaking of wind. But we can start with the kitchen."

"I don't work at that office anymore," said the Warlock. "I don't think the kitchen really matters anymore."

"Explain that."

"Mr. Foster had a talk with me about it yesterday. I feed strays this way and I was practicing on a sandwich and... look, I really don't know why it turned into a curse and keeps doing the transformations on its own. Mr. Foster said he'd give a good reference, but that today would be my last day."

"I don't think he's intending for this to be quite so friendly," said Mister Lewis. "Where'd you learn to turn carpet into a reflective surface and mimic the movements of its targets?"

"Oh, that wasn't me. I'm not really that advanced. I've only been doing this for a couple months."

"Let me guess. Dropped out of college?"

"No, I graduated early. I started learning magic to help me type faster. You can't really use dictation software if you don't have an office, so it seemed like the most efficient thing. And then, you know, feeding animals."

"You signed your termination papers and left?"

"No. He just told me this would be my last day. It's OK. Everybody there is kind of mean. I was thinking about looking for a new job anyway."

"And what about the fart noises in the office?"

"I don't really do audio. I/O interface manipulation for the typing, which is harder than it sounds and then I'm trying to learn basic transmogrification for food. I mean, everything else magic in the office is about women. I wouldn't know how to make gender trigger a conjuring."

"When you frame it that way, it does pose a question. By the way, what's the story with your Familiar?"

Mister Lewis gestured towards the stray beagle, which had finished its meal. It was shifting its gaze between Mister Lewis and the Warlock... and it seemed less mangy and larger than when it had entered the alley.

"I don't have a Familiar," replied the Warlock. "That's just a stray and... are his eyes glowing?"

The beagle's eyes were indeed glowing.

"That's not a dog," said Mister Lewis. "Come towards me slowly. We need to get out of the alley."

The Warlock took a step backwards toward the mouth of the alley and the dog started to change. Its limbs extended, the claws on its paws extended, its jaw extended and teeth with it. And then it spoke.

"Hey assholes," said the not-quite-dog. "I speak English, too."

And then it jumped on the Warlock.

The Warlock screamed as he fell backwards and the not-quite-dog's claws dug into his chest, but he managed to twist away from its snapping jaws.

Mister Lewis stepped into a kick and managed to get a foot between the Warlock and the creature, knocking the creature back a couple feet. As it tumbled, the creature continued to grow, looking more bipedal by the second.

"Get out of here and go to ground," Mister Lewis said to the Warlock. "Out of the city."

"You realize I can track him by smell, smart guy," said the creature as it stood on it hind legs and struck a pose that was either from a body building contest or a pro wrestling rerun. "Look at these muscles. They're going to beat you and then I'm going to eat you."

The Warlock ran.

"That trail of blood makes it even easier," called the creature after him.

Mister Lewis squared himself against the creature, which wasn't done posing. Never turn your back on something that might be able to outrun you, and it looked like it might be fast. It wasn't standing as tall as Mister Lewis and it wasn't thick, but the muscles were wiry and there were plenty of claws and teeth. It wasn't clear if this was going to be a fair fight, but it beat getting bitten in the back of the neck while trying to run away.

The creature charged, running like a man.

It probably would have outrun Mister Lewis, who slid right and stuck a knee into the creature's side as it went by. The claws on a paw raked his upper arm, cutting through the sleeve of his jacket and drawing blood, but the creature lost its balance and crashed into a dumpster.

As the creature collected itself, Mister Lewis reached down and picked up the Warlock's silver chain.

"How do you feel about enchanter's silver," Mister Lewis asked the creature.

The creature didn't reply.

"Thought so."

"Hard to use when you're dead," said the creature as it charged again.

Mister Lewis tossed the chain into the creature's face. Despite being a gentle toss born by the flick of a wrist, the chain took a chunk out of the creature's face and ruptured its right eye before falling to the ground.

The creature howled in pain as it dropped to one knee.

"Disrupts your form, doesn't it," Mister Lewis asked the creature which was trying to stand up, one paw over the ruptured eye. He leaned over and retrieved the silver chain.

As it stood up, Mister Lewis slipped the silver chain around its neck, pressed his knee into its back and pulled. Instead of garroting the creature, the silver chain slowly worked its way through its neck, dissolving the flesh like it was acid.

The creature flailed until the head fell off. It didn't bleed.

Mister Lewis tossed the head and torso in the dumpster and dropped a match in after them before shutting the lid.

Executive Summary Judgement

❧

"I've got good news and bad news," said Mister Lewis as he walked into the Human Resources office. "The good news is that your boy Charlie really is a Warlock."

"What happened to your arm," asked the woman from Human Resources, eyeing the torn sleeve and dried blood.

"That's the bad news. He really isn't any older than he looks and while he did cause the problem in the kitchen, he didn't have anything to do with your mirror problem. And something tried to eat him. He's not your only Warlock."

"But your arm?"

"Something tried to eat me, too. I have poor reactions when things try to eat me."

"That doesn't make sense," said the woman from Human Resources who was flashing the insincere smile again.

"Where's my C-HO," bellowed the CEO as he stuck his head in the door.

"The candidate is late for her interview," sighed the woman from Human Resources.

"Where's my Warlock," bellowed the CEO.

"Which Warlock," replied Mister Lewis. "You have more than one."

Before the CEO could respond, the color faded from the carpet and the reflections returned.

"That's it," screamed the woman from Human Resources. "Enough. Everyone out."

"Right," said the CEO, but before his head bobbed out of the doorway, Mister Lewis caught his reflection in the floor. The reflection of someone well over retirement age.

"I'll just go talk with Mr. Foster," said Mister Lewis, exiting with haste.

The CEO was in his clubhouse of an office sipping from his oversized silver chalice. The two brogrammers with the beer bong were still in their chairs, but they'd switched which one was on the receiving end of the bong.

"Would you like a magazine," asked the CEO, who held up an old issue of *Hustler*. "Print is so retro, and isn't it ironic we'd have it in the office?"

"You need to level with me about the youth thing," Mister Lewis approached the desk.

"It's in the management book and the investors prefer to fund by the book."

"No. When the mirrors lit up the HR office, I saw your face. Your real face. What's up with the youth thing?"

"Ah," sighed the CEO. "I suppose it takes one to know one."

"Let's just say I'm experienced in these matters. Why the charade?"

"Oh, it really is about the money. You've never heard investors talk about how they invest in the people, not the product? I'm just giving them the type of person they've been looking for. And for the last decade, they've been looking for scrawny college dropouts who resemble the one who struck it big. People can be so shallow."

"How long have you been running this scam?"

"This is my fourth persona. If you look the part and sign whatever they put in front of you, money falls from the sky. You overpay yourself, lavish yourself with perks, divert a little money into items that leave with you like this lovely silver cup and nobody looks very close when a startup fails. They usually want the founder to walk away rather than question why the deal he signed makes sure he's the only one who doesn't get paid in the breakup. Ride the wave, put on a new face, then ride again. And for once you're not worried about laundering your income. Besides, you can't beat startup culture for a good time. Do anything you want and nobody complains as long as they have aspirations of participating in an IPO. Wouldn't want to be banished for being a prude."

"So what was the deal with the Charlie kid," asked Mister Lewis.

"HR thought we might have a prude in the office, so we needed a scapegoat. He was obvious and handy. At least until I can do something about the prude. The Big Book of $tartup $uccess is very clear on this: no negative opinions can be permitted and you fire anyone who disagrees with you. Not that I need a book to tell me that, but it does make the lifestyle easier to maintain... I assume by the look of your arm, you saw what happened to Charlie. How much is this going to cost me?"

"Here's the thing," said Mister Lewis. "I take it personally when something tries to eat me. Also, the kid's alive. Your creature, not so much."

"You killed my Familiar," the CEO tilted his head as though in contemplation.

"Beheaded it, if you want to be specific. The remains are in a dumpster fire, but I'm guessing it burns easy and doesn't leave much ash."

The CEO tilted his head from left to right, lifted his right hand and gestured at Mister Lewis with two fingers. The two brogrammers dropped the beer bong and stood up.

"Those two are supposed to intimidate me," asked Mister Lewis.

"Why is it you think I only have one Familiar? If there's one thing I've learned from this tech business, it's the importance of redundant backups." The CEO snapped his fingers and the brogrammers started changing form, just like the dog creature in the alley.

Mister Lewis stepped back and drew the silver chain from his pocket, but has soon as it came free, it flew out of his hand across the room and fell in the far corner.

"That would explain a few things," said the CEO. "But let's play this round straight."

The Familiars charged.

Mister Lewis managed to catch the first Familiar with an elbow and knock it aside, but the second one hit him straight on and drove him into the wall next to the door.

He managed to get a forearm under the jaws and keep them pushed back an inch from his throat as they snapped.

Frustrated with its lack of chewing, the Familiar tossed Mister Lewis across the room towards the first Familiar. The first Familiar backhanded him and he crashed into the desk.

"I'm ready for an aperitif," the CEO stared down at Mister Lewis and took a sip from his silver goblet.

The first Familiar approached. It must have been excited as its teeth were dripping saliva like a leaky faucet. It growled and crept closer. The CEO stared down and grinned.

As the first Familiar was upon him, Mister Lewis reached up, snatched the silver goblet out of the CEO's hand and swung it hard at the first Familiar's head. The first Familiar's head caved and it fell to the ground with a goblet-shaped indentation in its skill.

The second Familiar howled and charged, but Mister Lewis met the charge by thrusting the goblet forward into its face, collapsing the upper jaw and burying the rim of the goblet three inches into the second Familiar's face, the way a child would press a bucket into the sand at the beach. He released the goblet and the second Familiar slumped to the floor.

"Fine," the CEO started to raise his arms, but before he could, Mister Lewis locked a hand around his throat.

"Be very careful what comes out of your mouth," said Mister Lewis. "I saw your true image and I don't think ancient Warlocks are as hardy as their Familiars."

"Mr. Foster, your interview is here," came the call of

the woman from Human Resources, who walked into the office accompanied by a young woman in a very short and very sparkly dress who could only be the VIP hostess being considered for Chief Hospitality Officer.

"He's a little busy," said Mister Lewis as he switched his hold from an open hand choke to lightly squeezing the throat with the crook of his other arm.

The color didn't fade from the floor, so much as the mirrored surface appeared in a flash.

The woman from Human Resources and the Chief Hospitality Officer candidate stared at the dead Familiars on the floor and the wizened reflection of the CEO.

"I think I'm having a flashback," stammered the Chief Hospitality Officer candidate.

"Perhaps you should go and we can reschedule," said the woman from Human Resources. Now her smile was sincere, but it still wasn't pleasant.

The Chief Hospitality Officer candidate left in a hurry.

The woman from Human Resources stepped forward as Mister Lewis dragged the CEO out from behind the desk and forced him down on his knees, face leaning towards the mirrored floor.

"Do you accept this as proof of the Warlock's identity," asked Mister Lewis, nodding towards the CEO's reflection.

"I do."

"Do you accept what you see here as documentation of infractions?"

"I do."

"Do you accept you have no job without me," growled the CEO.

"I wouldn't say that," said the woman from Human Resources, positively beaming. "You're hardly the first founder or CEO to get caught misbehaving. Line of succession steps are very clearly enumerated in The Big Book of $tartup $uccess. Oh, and I have the next most equity, don't I?"

"Is that why you wanted a consultant," the CEO eyes were wider in their reflection than in the youthful mask they wore outside it.

"I'm not an idiot," she replied. "All the perverts sit in your office. There were only four choices and they all were equity clawbacks. It was suspicious that Croker University didn't have admission records on you. Now it looks like all four pieces of equity will be returning to the company. I'm sure the investors will appreciate how I'm not just heading off a lawsuit, I'm also reclaiming value."

"I bet those investors are going to look closer at the dropouts after this," chuckled Mister Lewis. "It was nice while it lasted."

"No," the CEO's eyes grew wild and Mister Lewis tightened his grip around his neck. "Not this way."

"You had a different exit in mind," asked the woman from Human Resources.

"Yes," screamed the CEO. "Dust before dishonor."

The CEO suddenly shifted his weight forward, bringing himself and Mister Lewis to the floor. When his face came in contact with his reflection, the image of youth disappeared.

Then he turned grey.

Then he crumbled to dust.

"Does this change anything in that line of succession you were talking about," asked Mister Lewis as he brushed himself off.

"No, you'd be surprised how many founders and CEO's flake out and disappear," said the new CEO. "Not usually that kind of flaking, but that's also in the book. Everything will work out the way I wanted."

"In that case, you'll probably want to play it safe and scatter his dust. Those bodies will burn cleanly without residue. If our business is concluded, could I get a check for my fee? Procedures in the book or not, I think I'd like to cash it right away."

THE GENTRIFIED
BODEGA

A Renter and Her Missing Keys

❦

H eidi MacDonald pressed the buzzer for the third time and waited. Finally, the door buzzed open and she climbed three flights of stairs to her dream apartment. 800 square feet. Hardwood floors. An enormous antique bathtub on claw feet above checkered tiles. A double bowl sink and ample counter space in the kitchen. Two walk-in closets. All for far below market rent.

Heidi MacDonald was pissed when she knocked on the door of her dream apartment. A knock that wasn't answered, so she knocked again and waited.

The tiny sounds of shuffling feet could be heard inside the apartment, but the shuffling wasn't headed towards the door.

"Where are my keys," bellowed MacDonald as she started pounding on the door with a clenched fist. "You can't have an open house after you've cashed my deposit check."

The tiny sounds of shuffling continued.

"My keys or my money back," the blood was rushing to her cheeks as she kept hitting the door.

The shuffling sound came towards the door. The sounds of locks turning came from behind the door and it opened a crack.

"Hello," said MacDonald as she slowly pushed the door open a quarter of the way.

No one replied to her, so she hesitantly stuck her face into the opening between the door and the frame.

"Hello," she said again.

Much to her shock, MacDonald discovered she was eye to eye with an insect whose head was the same size as her own. The insect's proboscis pierced her face and took a sip of all the blood that had been coming to the surface in her rage. Then it dragged her into the apartment.

Heidi MacDonald was in her dream apartment for 2 minutes before she expired.

Clean Up In Aisle 3

An old man in a bright red coat with entirely too many buttons was trying to mop up the blood splatter in the back of the bodega. He smelled of liquor, but he didn't seem wobbly.

"That's where they found her," asked Mister Lewis.

"Correct," said Earl Lancaster, the new client. "There was blood on the fire escape in the alley. It looked like she was dragged from the top floor."

"Wounds consistent with bug bites, but too large," said Mister Lewis, examining a picture of the victim. "This can't be the only unusual thing if you called me."

"Just the most dramatic," Lancaster beckoned him away from the man with the mop and lowered his voice. "That woman was the third person who claims to have signed a lease for the top floor apartment. All three of them had a deposit check cashed and in all three, the bank's video surveillance shows me cashing it."

"Mysterious giant insect bites and a doppelganger,"

mused Mister Lewis. "I suppose it's unusual, but we'll have to see if it's unnatural."

Mister Lewis had a business card that said "Physics Consultant," but that title was a bit tongue-in-cheek. He consulted on matters where the laws of physics didn't apply and unnatural creatures were involved.

"The other me aside," Lancaster hissed, "this is pretty simple. I've got a deal in place to sell this building. The neighborhood's gentrified, so they're going to tear it down and put up 20 stories of condos with a yogurt store on ground level. It took forever to get the tenants out and the cops are holding up the sale. I need you to get rid of whatever's causing all this so I can cash out."

"Are you in danger of being arrested over the doppelganger?"

"No. I'm lawyered up and I've got iron clad alibis. The cops don't understand it, but they understand I wasn't in those banks cashing checks."

"What's the story with the bodega and the guy with the mop," asked Mister Lewis.

"The bodega isn't a problem. It was on a month-to-month lease before I bought the building. The old lush is the grandfather of the owner. Name's O'Mooney, like the sign out front. The owner used to live upstairs, but finally moved out when I raised the rent. He started showing up to run the place after his grandson moved out."

O'Mooney must've heard his name. He turned his head and half stumbled over to where Lancaster and Mister Lewis were huddled.

"I want to report that three bottles of whiskey were

stolen when the body showed up," said O'Mooney, a little too earnestly.

"Right," said Lancaster. "I'm sure you can fudge the paperwork for your insurance claim, but you probably should make it a little higher than three if you want to get ahead."

"I wouldn't want to be the only one not fudging the paperwork around here," replied O'Mooney.

Follow the Money

✲❀✲

The bank manager was only too happy to show Mister Lewis the video tape of Earl Lancaster cashing Heidi MacDonald's housing deposit check.

There it was in crisp black and white footage. Lancaster entered the bank, walked up to the teller, presented the check and an ID, then left. The teller's facial expression was a bit blank, but that was hardly conclusive. That could have been personality as easily as an unnatural influence. The picture was clear enough to rule out a disguise though. A doppelganger or a twin.

"Did Lancaster have an account here," Mister Lewis asked the manager.

"No, but his paperwork was in order both times," replied the manager.

"Both times?"

"Yes. That tape was from a week ago. He was also here yesterday. We had a customer come in trying to stop his check about an hour ago. That's when we realized he'd been here twice."

The surveillance tape of the second incident was pulled up and it was almost identical to the first tape.

"You have the photos of the identification he used," asked Mister Lewis.

"No," said the manager. "The cameras we use for those have been breaking, the last week."

Once more a convenient coincidence that couldn't be confirmed or ruled out. Although sometimes coincidence could be a trend unto itself.

"Would you be able to give me the phone number of this second customer," asked Mister Lewis.

"No," said the manager, "but under the circumstances, I can bend the rules a little. Call him myself and hand you the phone."

Flaming Angry

✿❀✿

"That's right," Tariq Zawahir said into his cell phone. "I signed a lease two days ago. And then I saw the news about the murder online today. Same apartment the dead lady signed a lease for. The ad for the place is still up on Newman's List."

"Did you notice anything unusual about the man showing you the apartment," asked Mister Lewis, speaking into the bank manager's phone.

"He was very interested in getting my money," replied Zawahir. "Offered me a discount if I'd pay in cash. I should've seen this coming."

"And it was the same man as in the surveillance video you saw in the bank," asked Mister Lewis.

"It was," replied Zawahir. "Which is good, because it means I know who I'm looking for and I'm going to get my money back."

"It may not be quite as simple as that," said Mister

Lewis. "There may be two different men who look the same."

"Oh, I'm not worried about that," replied Zawahir. "I made a new email address and arranged for a showing of that apartment. That fricking idiot will be there and when I lay hands on him, I will have my money before I let go of him. I'm about to walk into the place now."

"You don't want to do," Mister Lewis started to say, but Zawahir had already hung up.

Tariq Zawahir rung the bell. The door buzzed open and he climbed three flights of stairs to the front door of the apartment he'd thought was his.

Zawahir raised his hand to knock and noticed the door was open a crack. A grim smile passed his lips as he threw the door open hard enough it bounced back off the wall and hit his shoulder as he stormed in.

He opened his mouth to demand his money, but before a word could form he was enveloped in a column of flame.

Tariq Zawahir died without a refund on his apartment.

The Bodega That Has Everything

When Mister Lewis got out of the cab, there were police cars in front of the building and a commotion inside the bodega on the first floor. As he walked through the bodega's front door, he was hailed by O'Mooney. O'Mooney was hanging a sign above the cash register.

"Would you like to sell me some gold," asked O'Mooney as the left side of a "We Buy Gold" sign slipped into the hook he'd dropped from the ceiling.

"I don't think I've been to a bodega that buys gold before," said Mister Lewis.

"You change with the neighborhood," O'Mooney said with a mild slur to his speech. "The neighborhood's getting fancy and that means more jewelry and precious metals. And I'm happy to take it off their hands. Gold is the most reliable currency. It travels well. Never trust a currency that isn't on the gold standard."

There was a commotion in the back of the bodega as

a police forensics team was swarming around roughly the same place Heidi MacDonald's body was found. Lancaster, hovering over the scene, noticed Mister Lewis and scurried to the front of the room.

"Ah, Mr. Lancaster," O'Mooney greeted him. "Surely you have some gold for me."

Lancaster paused, glanced at O'Mooney, glanced at the sign about the register and made a face.

"This is serious," Lancaster growled. "There's a charred corpse in the back. Nobody knows who it is or how it got there."

"You sometimes get bodies when the neighborhood changes," O'Mooney said to Mister Lewis. "But not usually when the neighborhood gets fancy, though. Still... never let it be said O'Mooney's doesn't stock everything you could possibly want."

"They're probably going to discover his name is Tariq Zawahir," said Mister Lewis. "And then they're going to discover he also signed a lease for that fourth floor apartment. And then they're going to discover his deposit check was cashed yesterday and he had an appointment to have the apartment shown about 20 minutes ago."

"That body's only been there 20 minutes," offered O'Mooney. "He must've cooked fast."

"How did it get back there," asked Mister Lewis.

"I don't know," replied O'Mooney. "I was up here at the register and heard some noise. He was still flopping around a little for a couple minutes."

"What did the store security camera show?"

"I was thinking if I do well with the gold, I might buy

one of those," O'Mooney smiled broadly. His left eye looked out of focus.

"He's not the observant type," Lancaster took Mister Lewis by the arm and pulled him outside. "So I'm going to need another alibi? What time did that check get cashed this time?"

"About 1PM."

Lancaster froze up, closed his eyes and winced.

"You don't have an alibi for 1PM."

"Oh, no... I have an alibi," said Lancaster. "I was having a business lunch with the developer who's buying the building. Assuring him there was nothing to all the fake leases floating around and that we'd be able to finalize the transfer of deed soon. The last thing I want to do is get him involved with a... this is a murder, right?"

"It's hard to say how the police will end up classifying it," replied Mister Lewis, "but yes. This is looking personal and premeditated. Do you have any enemies?"

"I have tenants," said Lancaster. "Same difference most of the time. The Renter's Assistance Board. The Housing Department. Board of Supervisors. It comes with the business. But enemies that look like me and burn people alive? This isn't normal."

"No, nothing about this is normal. Someone or something has a bone to pick with you. Possibly literally. Is your developer likely to drop the deal if people have died in the building?"

"He could care less about bodies unless there's too much publicity and it affects the eventual condo sales. In this market, nobody's probably going to ask those kind of questions. The Poltergeist remake didn't do that well and nobody's building on a cemetery. At least I don't think there was ever a cemetery under the building. I could be wrong."

"You'd probably better call that developer and get your alibi in order. It's unlikely when I get to the bottom of this there will be an explanation suitable for the police."

Lancaster shook his head in a combination of resignation and disgust, then removed a cellphone from his pocket as he was walked away.

Mister Lewis turned and noticed O'Mooney gesturing to him from inside the bodega's front window.

"I've got a hot tip for you," O'Mooney said after Mister Lewis re-entered the store. "If you dig around, you'll find there's been a fire in the apartments before. Get it? Fire – hot tip?"

The Fine Art of Complaining

O'Mooney was half in the bag, but he wasn't off-base. With Lancaster convinced all his enemies were renters or people associated with renters' rights, a look at what complaints were registered was far from out of line. And there were plenty of complaints to be found through wonders of online records.

Lancaster had several buildings and the complaints ran the gamut from sloppy maintenance to a bit of housing discrimination. He had a penchant for arbitraging his real estate dollars by buying old buildings under rent control and finding creative ways to convince people to leave, thus being able to double or triple the rent for the new tenant. A tactic sure to make relatively few friends, with the possible exception of one renter who managed to figure out the apartment was cleared out by a false report that the original tenant was forced to vacate so that Lancaster's brother could move in. As no such person existed, let alone moved in, that renter was able to assume the 10 years of controlled rent rate of the renter who was evicted, so he probably was at least ambivalent towards Lancaster.

But the building where all hell was breaking loose, that one had a special set of calamities and complaints, all recent. The building originally had 6 apartments across 4 stories, with the bodega on the ground floor. The complaints from the top floor read like a soap opera.

There were originally 2 apartments on the top floor, most recently occupied by an Eric Hump and a Monty O'Mooney, who Mister Lewis took to be the owner of the bodega and grandson of the O'Mooney currently running the store.

Hump was evicted after a fire in his apartment. The cause of and responsibility for the fire were disputed. The eviction paperwork cited tenant negligence in starting the fire, which originated in the kitchen and mostly only caused smoke damage. Hump filed a complaint that the rest of his apartment had been disturbed and that someone had entered the apartment to cause the fire. Two conflicting opinions with little evidence either way, but Lancaster was lawyered up and Hump wasn't.

Then next complaint was that of an infestation. O'Mooney filed a complaint about bedbugs. After some prodding by the Housing Department, O'Mooney agreed to go on a vacation while exterminators took care of the bugs.

The complaint after that detailed O'Mooney

returning to find out that the wall between his apartment and the apartment formerly occupied by Hump had been torn down. Hump's kitchen and bathroom had been dismantled. The reward for the new layout? A mere 200% rent hike. While Lancaster couldn't seem to make up his mind for the official record whether it was now a two bedroom or three bedroom, (the issue of how to classify the former kitchen), he was very specific about how much should be charged for that floor, post-upgrades.

O'Mooney apparently moved out fairly quickly, rather than staying to contest.

The second floor had another eviction to make way for relative to move in. This time, it was supposed to be Lancaster's mother. It was likely that Lancaster at one time had a mother, although Mister Lewis wasn't entirely sure whether the mother was still alive. The remaining three apartments, while apparently vacant, had no outstanding paperwork filed against them. At least not that Mister Lewis could easily find.

"There are some things about your building's records we should talk about," Mister Lewis said into his phone.

"Records can be contested, but go ahead," replied Lancaster.

"How upset was Monty O'Mooney when he moved out?"

"Medium. He wasn't happy about the rent increase that came with the remodeling, but he saw the writing on the wall with his store's lease being about to end. Upset enough he let his grandfather run the store until we shut it down."

"Here's the thing," said Mister Lewis. "You've got a death that resembles insect bites and someone burned to death. You've got citations for a fire incident and a bug incident on that floor. That would be one helluva coincidence."

"Now look," Lancaster interjected. "There's a lot of hearsay about how that fire got started and the court said it was him, not me. And I can't possibly be responsible for somebody bringing home bedbugs. Those could have come from anywhere. I can't be accused..."

"I'm not making judgements," Mister Lewis returned the interjections. "At this point, it doesn't matter what the court ruled, it just matters that it happened and a pattern is taking shape. Although how it originally happened might make a difference if someone is basing a curse off it."

"No comment."

"Did your mother move into unit 301?"

"Let's just say she reserves the right to move in when she returns from Florida."

"How did 302 vacate?"

"Moved in with his boyfriend. Made him pay an early cancellation fee."

"And the second floor?"

"They, um... might have had some problems with the gas not working. It happens like that sometimes."

Mister Lewis paused to exhale.

"It would not be good if a gas leak met a burning body," said Mister Lewis.

"That's a tough one," replied Lancaster. "On the one

hand, I might not be able to charge as much if there's nothing left on the lot. On the other hand, that developer really only wants the lot and it might end up costing him less for the teardown. Probably would depend on the media spin. Could be a win-win."

The Real Estate Tour

Lancaster was not overly enthused to meet Mister Lewis for a room by room inspection of the apartments. Particularly now with the question of whether his apartments' gas problems might be fodder for a curse and the whole place could conceivably explode.

Despite their fears, the second floor of the building appeared to be empty and clean. There was no smell of gas, although Lancaster honestly couldn't remember if he'd had it turned back on. The apartments had some settled dust, but the dust was undisturbed. No one had been moving around in either apartment for some time.

Mister Lewis and Lancaster climbed the stairs to the third floor. Apartment 302 was much like the second floor apartments: empty with a bit of dust. Apartment 301 was different.

When Lancaster opened to door to 301, he found the apartment furnished.

"This shouldn't be in here," Lancaster said, glancing around to take in the couch, coffee table and recliner decorating the living room.

"Looks like the kitchen is full," said Mister Lewis, peering through the doorway. "Is it possible somebody moved in without you knowing?"

"Nothing that's happened this week is possible," grumbled Lancaster. "And this furniture looks familiar for some reason."

"Looks like the bedroom's furnished, too," said Mister Lewis.

The pair of them walked into the bedroom to find a bed, a nightstand, a dresser and a shipping box lying on the floor that was a bit over five feet long and two feet high.

"The bed's made," said Mister Lewis, "but I don't see any evidence of anyone living here. It's too neat. Like a showroom."

"What's with the giant cardboard box," asked Lancaster. "That's the only thing that's not furniture."

The two of them leaned over to examine the box. Three layers of packing tape traced the edges and seams, but it was pristine. There were no dents, scuffs or signs of having been shipped.

"Was this thing shipped or getting ready to be shipped," asked Lancaster.

"One way to find out," replied Mister Lewis, producing a pocket knife. "This smells like something's rotting inside. Anybody in this building have pets?"

"No pets allowed."

Mister Lewis sliced through the tape at the end of the

box. Enough to pry the corner up and peek in. The odor got worse as the corner lifted.

"I think that's somebody's foot," said Mister Lewis. "You might want to back into the living room. You don't want to be in here if this is a body and it animates."

"You mean somebody left me a zombie," stammered Lancaster.

"Or a wight. Or a wraith. Or just a corpse. You want to back up. This isn't how they're usually stored, but it might be about to get worse."

"Wouldn't it be better to just burn it," asked Lancaster.

"Only if it starts moving."

Keeping the box at arm's length, Mister Lewis slowly cut the tape around the edges and lifted the lid free.

Nothing moved.

The box contained the body of a slightly over-dressed woman surrounded by Styrofoam peanuts. She looked to have been about 80 when she died and there weren't any marks or bruises immediately visible.

"It's a just a corpse," Mister Lewis called out to Lancaster, who was hovering in the living room. "There's a note on its chest. 'Looks like she moved in after all. Does that save you a suit?' Mean anything to you?"

Lancaster, entered the doorway with a wrinkled brow and froze. Color drained from his face.

"You recognize her," said Mister Lewis.

"That's not possible," whispered Lancaster. "She's in Florida."

"Who's in Florida?"

"My Mother."

Lancaster backed away from the doorway and bumped into the couch.

"Oh no," Lancaster groaned. "That's why it looked familiar. This is her couch in Florida. How the hell did it get here?"

"We don't know if Hell was involved," said Mister Lewis. "That's not out of the question, though. Look, I still need to inspect the top floor. I don't think you want to go up there. Go downstairs to the bodega and wait for me."

"Are we going to call the police?"

"I don't know yet. Go downstairs."

Lancaster went downstairs and Mister Lewis went upstairs. The door to the floor's now sole apartment was ajar. Mister Lewis gently pushed it open with the extended index finger of his left hand. It wasn't dusty like the second floor apartments, but it was just as empty.

Mister Lewis stepped into the apartment, leaving the door ajar. He moved inwards and looked into the kitchen. Empty. He moved down the hall to the bedroom. Empty. He stepped further down the hall to the bathroom. Empty. This was where the wall separating what had been the second apartment on the floor had been torn down. As he took a step across the threshold of the former wall, the back of his neck began to tingle as though he was being watched.

Mister Lewis turned around. There was nothing there. Or was there?

He thought he saw something moving on the floor. He did. It was a bug. And it was getting bigger.

Shuffling towards him, now the size of terrier and still

growing was a bedbug. Not a starving one, either. The swollen blood red abdomen meant it had been feeding on someone.

Mister Lewis ducked in the bathroom and shut the door.

Something was hitting the door, and hitting it a little higher on the frame with each hit.

Looking around, the bathroom was bare. Bathtub. Sink. Toilet.

Lacking a better improvised weapon, Mister Lewis picked up the cover from the toilet tank and held the heavy ceramic piece above his head like a club.

The door buckled a little. Then it fell in. Climbing over it was a now man-sized bedbug.

Mister Lewis swung the toilet tank cover down the bedbug's head. The cover shattered with the hit but the bedbug went down, head hitting the toilet, momentarily stunned.

Mister Lewis pressed the advantage and took advantage of "normal" physics. With the bedbug's head on the toilet bowl and off the ground, he started stomping at its thorax, the segment between the head and abdomen.

The thorax caved and the head separated, knocking the toilet loose from the wall and causing a water leak. Then the abdomen started to leak the blood the bedbug had been feeding on. The blood mixed with the water to make swirling patterns as the floor flooded and started to drain into a hole in the wall behind where the toilet had been.

Mister Lewis pushed the abdomen segment back

with his foot and produced a penlight from his pocket. Shining the light into the hole, it appeared to be deeper than expected and would've been where the two apartments were originally divided. And there was something metallic reflecting light back at him.

Sticking his arm in the hole, he pulled out two large, curved pieces of a strange black metal. The pieces, when held together, seemed to form some sort of old-fashioned crock or kettle, but at least one piece was missing. He looked at the metal again and recognized it. Unlike separating the bug's head, this was not normal physics. But it did explain a few of the thing that had been happening.

He took the pieces and crawled over the abdomen that was partially blocking the door.

The Thing at the End of the Rainbow

"I pay top dollar for the gold," O'Mooney said to Lancaster. "I know you've got some. Let's make a deal. Get the gold's weight off your shoulders."

Lancaster just shook his head no. He looked like he might faint and he almost did when Mister Lewis entered the bodega. That was partially due to the blood that had gotten smeared on him crawling out of the bathroom, however.

"Those really were giant bedbug bites that killed Heidi MacDonald," Mister Lewis. "Enlarged and ensorcelled bedbugs, to be precise about it."

"Did you make an offering to the house spirit," interjected O'Mooney. "It can help with things like that."

"House spirit," Mister Lewis repeated. "Interesting jacket you have there. Seven buttons in each row?"

"Aye," said O'Mooney. "And seven rows. I thought you'd be one to be aware of his surroundings."

"Why leave the house spirit an offering of whiskey

when he's already offered it to himself," Mister Lewis stepped up to the counter and looked O'Mooney in the eye.

"Well, it's not like I can actually get drunk," O'Mooney said with a sigh. "My kind can only go halfway. But you knew our hands are always steady."

"What are you talking about," Lancaster mumbled.

"He's been hiding in plain sight," Mister Lewis replied, dropping the two pieces of metal he'd found in the wall onto the counter. "The red coat and buttons should have been obvious, but it didn't click until I found that in his grandson's bathroom."

"I would like to know how it was broken," O'Mooney piped in.

Mister Lewis and O'Mooney both turned to stare at Lancaster.

"Oh," Lancaster started to reply and then paused to gather his thoughts. "Probably just something that got broken when we were taking out the adjoining bathroom."

"This isn't the time for games," said Mister Lewis. "Did you take something out of the pot?"

"Oh, he did," O'Mooney assured him. "And he's been carrying it on him ever since. I can tell these things."

"Am not," Lancaster was starting to recover from his shock.

"Mister Lancaster," began Mister Lewis. "Look at that metal. It's the wrong color and texture. It comes from Fairie. What did you take? We may be able to end this very quickly."

"Oh, for the love of Mike," groaned O'Mooney. "Will this give you a clue?"

He waved hand and he was suddenly only two feet tall and standing on the counter next to the register.

Lancaster stared at him blankly.

"Hello? Leprechaun talking," shouted O'Mooney. "Now give me the damn gold."

"But... you're not wearing green," stammered Lancaster.

O'Mooney howled in frustration.

"Yeah, the whole green stereotype is kind of a Disney thing," said Mister Lewis. "But he's a Leprechaun all right and if you took his gold, that means you've got some wishes coming."

Magic wishes were apparently something Lancaster could process, or perhaps it was just the idea of getting something for free. Either way, he stuck a hand into his pocket and pulled out a fistful of gold coins.

"I wish I never have to follow the housing code again," Lancaster said with the enthusiasm normally reserved for New Year's Eve toasts.

"That's my grandson's gold," said O'Mooney with a sigh. "I'm not bound if it's someone else's gold. I had him clear out before old clueless there could extort any wishes. And I'm not sure I'd grant him wishes if it were mine, rules or no. 'Earl Lancaster.' An Englishman taking on airs of nobility. I've had quite enough of that over the years. Hand it over."

Mister Lewis turned towards O'Mooney, only to take a quick step back as another bedbug started growing to unusual size on the counter next to O'Mooney.

"He dropped more than one bedbug in my grandson's apartment," O'Mooney said a little too calmly as two more bedbugs sprung up behind Lancaster, blocking the door. "Look at the flat, brown bellies on them. They must be hungry. And let's not forget the fire our dear landlord set."

A column of flame blinked in and out of existence next to Lancaster.

"But you were right," O'Mooney nodded towards Mister Lewis. "This is all going to be over quickly. Hand over that gold and I'll be on my way. It doesn't belong to you. Otherwise..."

"Just like that," asked Mister Lewis.

"Just like that. I don't care to do business with the likes of him."

Lancaster stared at the coins in his hand before speaking.

"I thought I was paying you to make him go away."

"He is going to go away," replied Mister Lewis. "But if I do it the hard way, I don't think he's going to let you walk out of here."

A column of flame popped up next to Lancaster again and this time it didn't wink out.

Lancaster tossed the fistful of coins at O'Mooney. Somehow they all fell into the pocket of his coat. For the next three minutes, Lancaster was pulling coins from his pockets and throwing them with increasing force. Each time, the coins would land softly in O'Mooney's pocket.

"Now before I leave," began O'Mooney, "I should tell you I've done something in preparation for tonight. You like to use lawyers on your tenants, so I've... moved some things through legal channels. I've arranged for this building to go on the National Register of Historic Places. You're going to want to restore the top floor to how you found it. Save yourself some penalties. And forget about tearing it down now. You should be getting the paperwork on that tomorrow. Congratulations."

And then O'Mooney disappeared. The column of fire blinked out and the bedbugs returned to normal size. Mister Lewis ground the bug that had been staring at him hungrily under his heel.

"He's gone," said Mister Lewis, who walked to door, but paused before exiting. "Per our agreement, his departure concludes our business."

"But the horror is just beginning," said Lancaster.

STUDENT LOANS, PAID
IN BLOOD

Service with a Sneer

❧❦❧

"**C**an I confirm who I'm talking to?"

Josh Elder loved his new job with Consolidated Student Solutions. It paid better than his old job, he could play at being in the finance industry and everything had a script, so he didn't even have to think.

"Chuck Marsdale," came the reply from his telemarketer's headset.

"How can I help you today, Mr. Marsdale?"

"I need to get my student loan payments adjusted to my income level. I just can't afford them."

"Consolidated Student Solutions acquired your loan from Whatabank Student Loans in the form of a trust, so we can only offer you forbearance or an opportunity to become current after you've missed 4 consecutive payments."

"But I already used my forbearances," croaked

Marsdale. "And I'm only one month behind. Why can't we discuss an income adjustment?"

"I'm afraid the terms of that trust," Elder double checked the script, "legally prevent us from discussing any alternate arrangements. You could always refinance your loan. That could lower your monthly payment."

"I owe $75,000 and I have a minimum wage job."

"Let's see," Elder keyed the numbers into his computer. "No, you actually owe $96,000. During the forbearance period, your interest was added back onto your loan's principal. Will you be able to make this month's payment?"

"No, of course not. I just said I was already behind."

"After the fourth month, you'll be given an opportunity to catch up, but until then your interest will be added back onto your loan's principal, just as during the forbearance periods."

"If I've already used my forbearance and I don't have a good paying job, what I am supposed to do?"

"Well," Elder again double checked his script, "Consolidated Student Solutions encourages all its customers to practice responsible financial planning and use the tools made available to them like forbearance."

Marsdale hung up.

"Another satisfied customer," Elder said to himself, basking in the joys of following company policies.

The rest of his afternoon went much the same way: time spent helping people in their hour of need. At 5PM, he gave thanks for the rigidness of the banker hours that let him out of the office and started mentally planning his trip to the local watering hole where he would loosen his tie and attempt to lure over some recent liberal arts grads with the promise of buying them drinks they almost certainly couldn't afford with their coffee house jobs.

He got two blocks from his office before someone hailed him.

"Aren't you Josh Elder?"

Elder turned and saw an early twentysomething man in a fedora hat, a vest with no shirt underneath it, ripped jeans and a heavily waxed mustache.

"That's right," replied Elder.

"Does my voice sound familiar," asked the hipster.

"Should it?"

"We talked today," said the hipster.

Elder stood frozen. Nobody had ever shown him a script for this scenario and he wasn't sure what to do.

"You said I should practice responsible financial planning," said the hipster.

"Everyone should," Elder attempted a shit-eating grin.

"Do you think I can get blood out of this stone," asked the hipster as he raised his right hand, revealing a smooth stone about the size of a baseball in his palm.

"Um, no?"

"No," agreed the hipster. "So let's see if I can get blood with the stone, instead."

Elder's eyes tracked that stone as the arm swung and it approached his face. His eyes crossed just before it hit the space between them and then everything went black.

Know Your Customers

❧✦❧

"None of it makes any sense," Pat Penurious tried to explain. Penurious was the CEO of Consolidated Student Solutions and explaining the unexplained was usually pushed off on expendable junior executives.

"Start with the facts and we'll work out from there," said Mister Lewis. Mister Lewis specialized in things that didn't make any sense. His business card said "physics consultant," but he helped companies fix problems that defied the laws of physics and existed on a different plane of reality.

"This is the seventh business day in a row one of our customer service reps has failed to show up for work," began the CEO. "The first five are now officially missing persons. Three days after the employee disappears, a money order arrives to pay off the loan of a customer the employee spoke with the day of their disappearance."

"Do loans usually get paid off by money order?"

"Loans don't normally get paid off at all when people are calling about late payments," the CEO's face darkened. "Our business model isn't about loans being paid off early, either. This disrupts profits, as well as staffing. I need to know how this is happening and what this hipster from hell's game is."

"Hipster from hell," asked Mister Lewis.

"A hipster is behind this," said the CEO. "Maybe all the hipsters. There are witnesses with hazy recollections of seeing some of our missing employees talking to a hipster before disappearing."

"Hazy recollections?"

"That's just it, they can't remember exactly what the hipster looked like. Just that there was a hipster. And the employees just drop off any video footage before disappearing. I get that all hipsters look alike, but you'd think they'd remember something."

"So there may be a phantom hipster," mused Mister Lewis. "There's more to it?"

"And everyone who paid off their loan was a hipster," said the CEO.

"How do..." began Mister Lewis.

"I'll show you," interrupted the CEO.

The CEO gestured to a table on the left of Mister Lewis. On it were printouts of social media profiles, posts and especially pictures.

"These are customers who suddenly paid off their loans. Look at them. Hipsters. Disaffected, underemployed hipsters with terrible credit."

"Do you always keep records of your customers' social media accounts," asked Mister Lewis.

"It's a free country," said the CEO. "And sometimes it helps the collections department find people. And they're all in the same neighborhood with the rest of the hipsters over the bridge. Really, there's no way any of them could have paid their loans legitimately. This isn't natural."

"I suppose that neighborhood is a good place to start," said Mister Lewis. "And I suppose I have some idea who I'm looking for with all this. We'll have to see how natural or unnatural the explanation is."

It's Like Money Grows on Trees

So Mister Lewis went over the bridge to the land of the hipsters. And what he found was a block party. Drunken twentysomethings in the street, drinking and singing under banners that read "Lord of Irony."

Mister Lewis wasn't quite sure if "Lord of Irony" was a band or a slogan, but adding black sunglasses to his black suit was close enough to the formal wear side of hipsterdom to mingle without drawing more than a minor amount of attention.

It wasn't that unusual, as far as block parties went. Only two things stood out as different. The first was the lack of a band. The second was the passing around of what looked to be gold coins. Everyone was cagey about what it was that was getting passed around. It would get put away before Mister Lewis could get close enough for a good look. He fit in just well enough not to be asked to leave, but he clearly wasn't a familiar face. People were talking about gold, though. Exchange rates for gold. The best place to sell gold. How many pounds of gold it would take to pay off a loan.

If there wasn't a buzz in the crowd about paying off loans with gold, the rest of it very easily could have been a late night infomercial. The only thing missing was the envelope to mail the gold away and get a check in return. Although this crowd seemed to have done a bit too much research on the whys and wherefores of selling to choose that option.

After a half an hour of trying to mingle and mostly getting mildly confused looks, a crowd started to form at the end of the block across from the park. Underneath the largest "Lord of Irony" banner stood a young man in a jazz age suit with a bowler hat and an out of place armlet that appeared to be made of silver wrapped around his left bicep. Mister Lewis recognized him from the social media printouts as Lance Gildersleave, the first person to have mysteriously paid off his student loan by money order after speaking with a now missing customer support rep.

"Attention everyone," called Gildersleave. "It's time."

As the crowd continued to gather, Mister Lewis noticed two more faces behind Gildersleave. Three people who paid off their loans after their customer service rep disappeared, all seemingly in charge of the same block party? It wasn't clear exactly what that meant, but it definitely was stretching anyone's definition of coincidence pretty thin.

"We're glad you could join us," continued Gildersleave. "We've all come to love the Lord of Irony and we think you will love him, too. We want you to experience his act of love for yourself. Please, follow us into the park and into the grove. We think it will change your life."

With that, Gildersleave and his friends turned and walked into the park. Most of the crowd followed them.

Mister Lewis really wasn't sure what to expect from this "Lord of Irony." It sounded like a good name for a band and this was the right crowd for that. On the other hand, Gildersleave had been referring to this "lord" as though he were a person. "Experience his act of love." This wasn't going to be an orgy? He'd probably have to charge Consolidated Student Solutions extra if that were the case.

The group trudged through the park and into a forested section. Not far into the forest, sure enough, there was a grove. Everyone got very quiet when they entered the grove. Mostly out of shock.

Hanging from the trees by their heels were seven people. They were trussed up like meat in the butcher shop, throats slashed and a bit of blood spatter on the ground underneath them. They had been bled out, as though they were being prepared as food.

"The Lord of Irony loves us and wants us to prosper," droned Gildersleave as he paraded in front of the hanging bodies. "Many of you have student loans. This is the staff of Consolidated Student Solutions."

A smattering of jeers and hissing sprung up from the crowd.

"I know," continued Gildersleave, trying to quiet the crowd. "They used to hold my loan, too. But the Lord of

Irony provided for me. The Lord of Irony thought that Consolidated Student Solutions should pay for my loan."

Another young man wearing a vest with no shirt and a fedora hat approached Gildersleave. In his right hand, he held a long hunting knife. In his left hand, he held a copper bowl.

"Brother Marsdale has students loans he can't afford to pay," crooned Gildersleave. "The Lord of Irony shall provide for him. Watch and learn."

It was then that Mister Lewis realized one of the bodies didn't have a slashed throat. Gildersleave and Marsdale approached the man. He was suspended in air upside down with his head at about shoulder height on the hipsters.

It dawned on Mister Lewis what was about to happen, but he'd filtered in at the back of the crowd and there was no way he could get through them in time.

First Gildersleave grabbed the man's head by the hair and pulled down to steady it. Marsdale positioned the copper bowl under the man's head and a bit to right.

"Be careful not to spill any," said Gildersleave.

At this point, the hair pulling and the commotion woke up Josh Elder, who opened his eyes to see that hipster with the rock staring him right in the eyes. Only he was upside down and had a knife instead of a rock. Elder opened his mouth to speak, but before he get a word out, the hipster stabbed him in the throat and life started leaking out of him.

Marsdale moved his bowl to catch the greater portion of the blood that gushed out of Elder's neck. It was a bit of a mess and there was a clanging sound from the bowl, which seemed to be filling up quickly.

After about a minute, the bowl must have filled up, because the blood was now falling off it on onto the ground.

Marsdale turned and tilted the bowl to show the crowd. It looked like it was filled with gold. Then he dumped half of its contents onto the ground. It looked like gold coins. Gildersleave leaned over and picked one up.

"When they bleed us for the loans, they bleed us dry," cried Gildersleave. "But when we bleed them for the Lord of Irony, they bleed gold and we use that gold to pay off our loans. Can you feel our Lord's love?"

The crowd murmured mostly in confusion.

"Can the Lord of Irony ease your burden, too," Gildersleave rephrased the question.

This time the response was more positive.

"When the Lord of Irony feels enough love, he will appear," Gildersleave called, making a pantomime of a scout peering into the distance.

Mister Lewis was torn between waiting to see what this Lord of Irony looked like and getting the hell out of there before anyone noticed he didn't belong, since he wasn't completely sure what he'd walked into. Discretion won out.

Mister Lewis took two steps backwards and bumped into something bigger than him.

"You weren't on the guest list, magician," said a quiet, but familiar voice behind him.

Mister Lewis turned to see a tall man with flowing red

hair and a long, thick beard. He wore a massive fur coat, skinny jeans and a disingenuous t-shirt that read "I Am Not A Hipster." Flames danced on his brow where his eyebrows should have been, for this was Loki, the last survivor of Asgard in his preferred human form.

There was a flash of lightning after which neither Mister Lewis nor Loki were still standing there.

Tea and Civil Conversation

❦

When Mister Lewis regained his vision after the lightning flashed, he discovered he was no longer in the grove. He was back in the hipster neighborhood, just outside where the block party had been. He and Loki were seated at the same table in a sidewalk café and they had cups of tea in front of them.

"Really magician," said Loki. "I do like you, but this is not the best time for a visit."

"How did you do that," asked Mister Lewis.

"I am a god," replied Loki, "and you really didn't want to be there."

"Why? Were your children going to sacrifice me?"

"My children," Loki snickered. "No, those children were mortal like you. Would they have sacrificed you? That depends. It wouldn't be ironic to sacrifice you unless you were servicing their loans. Are you servicing their loans, magician?"

"Isn't a murder cult a little high profile for you?"

"A murder cult," this time Loki fully committed to laughter. "This is why I like having you around. Is that what you think it is?"

"Sure looked like a murder to me."

"Oh, come on," said Loki. "You can't start a new religion without a little spilt blood."

Mister Lewis stared at him instead of replying.

"You Americans are so myopic," Loki rolled his eyes. "Did you learn nothing from Greece? Financial ruin? Youths with a bad attitude about not having jobs?"

"Pray enlighten me," said Mister Lewis.

"Exactly," said Loki. "Praying for enlightenment is exactly what they're doing. Much as with Greece, your youths are feeling the squeeze of a financial meltdown. Here it's not the banks melting down, at least for the moment, it's the student loans melting down those children. They can't pay. They get desperate. Then I offer them a solution that fits into their culture."

"And you've added 'Lord of Irony' to your titles," asked Mister Lewis.

"God of wildfire, god of tricksters, god of disguises, god of misdirection... why not god of irony, too?"

"You always were humble."

"See," laughed Loki, "I'm god of sarcasm, too. I've inspired you. Your banks have dealt these children a hand from a deck that's been stacked against them. Just stay off in your own corner and let this little experiment run its course. You're right. This is more of a public display than I usually make, but given your country's pending student loan meltdown and all your bankers determined to make Odin seem like a forgiving authority figure, this is a chance for me to be a major religion again. These opportunities don't just grow on trees. Not even on Yggdrasil. Although I harbor some doubts about these children's ability to properly follow the rituals. They're a bit too independent. You can't be lax about the rituals when starting up a new religion. Bad form."

"That would be terrible," said Mister Lewis.

"Facilitating a trade is serious business," Loki's eyes narrowed and his brows flickered a bit higher. "The trade of blood even moreso. You know our business, magician. There are rules to be observed. Even by me."

"Yes, murder cults are a serious business."

"Oh, be that way," Loki scowled. "If this experiment works, you might find there are benefits to knowing a more popular god. I'm sure I can find some work for you. Final warning: walk away."

There was another flash of lightning and Loki's chair was empty.

"Walk away," muttered Mister Lewis. "Maybe if you didn't owe me money..."

Rates of Exchange

❦

Mister Lewis made his way back to the edge of the park to see the crowd starting to emerge from it and disperse. The show was over and the looks on the faces of those who had attended ran the gamut from shocked to giddy. Which seemed like an overall win for Loki's experiment.

Straggling along at the end was Marsdale, still clutching his bowl of gold coins and accompanied by another young twentysomething man with a pencil-thin mustache and a man bun. They separated off from the crowd and headed into the commercial district.

Mister Lewis followed at a distance and watched them go into a jewelry shop. No great mystery what they were doing there, since that was apparently what everyone at the block party had been talking about. Sure enough, they emerged fifteen minutes later with Marsdale holding the empty sacrificial bowl under one arm and carrying a brown paper bag in the other. Mister

Lewis wondered if carrying enough money to pay off a student loan in a brown paper bag was considered ironic in this neighborhood. In some cities it was the standard way for paying off aldermen, but he wasn't sure this crowd would be aware of it.

The next stop was at a check cashing store. Again, not a surprise. The money orders had to come from somewhere and it didn't require a close eye. Nor did their immediately proceeding to a mailbox and dropping an envelope into it. Once the sacrifice had been made, everything had proceeded more or less the way you'd expect after what the CEO had described.

Then the two hipsters walked into a bar. Despite it feeling like the setup to a joke, Mister Lewis followed them in and took a seat close enough to listen.

"Free at last," said Marsdale before slamming a shot.

"There has to be a better was to do this," said his friend with the man bun.

"And how do you propose to do that in a gig economy," asked Marsdale. "Nobody hires fulltime anymore. Especially not artists. They all contract it out and the temp agencies are so busy trying to underbid each other there's nothing left over after. And that's if you can make rent that month."

"I know, I know," groaned his friend with the man bun. "But human sacrifice for loan payments? That's... not normal. It's creepy."

"No, it's human sacrifice to pay completely pay off the loan," said Marsdale. "Don't sell it short. The Lord of Irony isn't asking us to do it every month like the loan companies do."

"Yeah, but what does he get," asked his friend with the man bun. "There's got to be a catch. It's not just blood for gold is it? Are you sure you didn't just sell your soul to pay off your loan?"

"Pick your poison," said Marsdale. "You need to look at this situation pragmatically. What happens when you can't pay your loan at the end of the month?"

"They hit my credit rating."

"Oh, like that even makes a difference after the last year?"

"True that."

"Let me tell you what they do," said Marsdale. They take all that interest from this month and they stick it back on the principal. That loan's only, what, three years old? They're probably sticking $400 bucks back on your loan. And then you pay interest on that $400, along with everything else. It's compound interest working against you."

"Can't pay the loan without a better job," replied his friend with the man bun. "Can't refinance the loan without a better job, either. It's a goddamn trap."

"That's exactly what it is," said Marsdale. "The stark reality of it is that Consolidated Student Solutions already owns your soul. They own all of you. Lock, stock and barrel. They've got you boxed in where you can't afford your payments, you're not allowed to renegotiate them and you're not allowed to declare bankruptcy. You just get to fall further and further in debt. Watch them try and pass a law where your children inherit the loan when you die. You know somebody's thinking about it."

The friend with the man bun groaned again, clearly not having any trouble picturing that.

"If I just traded my soul to the Lord of Irony, and I don't know whether or not I did," continued Marsdale, "here's the pragmatic way to look at it: I already sold my soul to the loan company, so I'm just swapping out owners. It's pretty clear which owner is actually trying to help me. Hell, the ritual is evidence of that."

"How's that again?"

"Dude, you need to pay attention," said Marsdale. "You have to follow the ritual or there's no irony to it. First you call Consolidated Student Solutions for help with your loan. Then they'll refuse you because, well... when was the last time they actually helped someone? Then we snatch whoever refused to help you."

"How do we find them again?"

"It's magic, dude. We just do and you'll know their face when you see it. That's why he's the Lord of Irony."

"I... guess," the friend with the man bun paused in thought. "I guess you have a valid point. We're all damned if we do and damned if we don't. At least we can put off being damned a little while longer."

"Exactly," Marsdale smiled. "There's only one choice with any upside to it. And here's the really interesting part. This ceremony is supposed to go eight days. I think the head of the snake is going to answer the phone when you call tomorrow and then we get to cut off the head."

"You mean... literally?"

"Maybe? That would just be a deeper cut than we've been making. If it happens, just get the bowl right under the neck stump. There could be blood everywhere and you're not getting any gold out of blood that's already hit the ground."

"More rules?"

"That's how the ritual's supposed to work. Haven't tried it, don't wanna find out. But at the end of eight days, the Lord of Irony will call down the lightning to burn down the grove and it will burn so hot, there won't be anything left. No evidence. We just move on debt free."

The pair ordered another round as Mister Lewis slipped off his stool and headed for the door. If the ritual called for the "head of the snake," he had an idea who the snake was and it wasn't going to be an easy sell to make the snake go into hiding.

Snake Charming

✦

"That's ridiculous," said Pat Penurious, CEO of Consolidated Student Solutions. "Nobody does blood sacrifice anymore. That's what campaign contributions are for."

"You hired me because you thought something unnatural was going on," Mister Lewis took a sip of coffee. "You were right. It's a murder cult with a mad god backing them. If you go into the office today, you're going to get a phone call and you're going to get dragged into the ritual. Possibly beheaded."

Mister Lewis had managed to convince the CEO to meet him in a coffee shop before going into work. It was ironic that the CEO would hire him to root out an unnatural threat, only to not believe such a thing was really happening and Mister Lewis was highly suspicious of anything ironic after the previous day's events.

"Shouldn't we call the police if there are bodies," asked the CEO.

"You don't want anybody disturbing the ritual while it's active," replied Mister Lewis. "The ritual wants you. The ritual needs to be completed today. All we have to do is get you far away from these people until midnight. If the ritual isn't finished on time, the magic will dissipate and Loki will start pouting. It will buy me some time to clean this up without risking more fallout. If you land in the middle of the ritual, I can't guarantee your safety. We're talking the affairs of gods, not a shambling zombie. It's a lot easier to outrun a zombie."

"I could buy that a bunch of hipsters would rather murder than pay their loans," said the CEO. "I could maybe buy they had some kind of Ouija board to find their customer service reps. Blood turning to gold? No. That I can't buy."

The CEO stood up from the table.

"I need to get to the office," said the CEO. "Business doesn't wait for hipsters."

"That's a bad idea," Mister Lewis started to say, but was interrupted by the CEO's cell phone ringing. "Do not answer that."

"Penurious," the CEO answered anyway.

"Hi," said the voice on the phone. "I can't afford my loan payments. Can you help me?"

Pat Penurious stared at the phone and hung up without saying a word.

"That was somebody about their student loan, wasn't it," asked Mister Lewis.

"When I get to the office, I'll find out how a call got transferred to my cell," answered the CEO. "It will not happen again."

The CEO stormed out of the coffee shop. Mister Lewis followed.

The CEO only got 8 steps past the front door before being confronted by a group of hipsters.

"Do you recognize my voice," said the hipster in front of the group, a twentysomething man with a pencil-thin mustache and a man bun.

"Get a job," said the CEO, not breaking stride.

"There's a better way to pay than getting a job," said the hipster with the man bun.

"Run," Mister Lewis hissed as he jumped in front of the CEO and cocked his fist to take a swing at the hipster with the man bun.

Before he could swing, a floating image of Loki's head flickered into existence between Mister Lewis and the hipsters.

"You were warned to stay away," said Loki's visage.

"I knew it," screamed the CEO. "There's a hipster from hell behind all this."

Then there was a lightning flash and everyone vanished.

Substantial Penalty for Early Withdrawal

❧

When his vision cleared, Mister Lewis realized he was back in the grove. A now-familiar troupe of eight hipsters was in the process of hanging the CEO upside down next to the bodies of the customer staff.

"It will all be over soon," said Lance Gildersleave, clearly the alpha hipster of the group. "Just pretend the last hour didn't happen. That was just our Lord of Irony aiding us."

"Yeah, but that guy was heavy," whined Marsdale as he glanced in the direction of Mister Lewis. "And it looks like he's awake."

Mister Lewis realized that he'd been bound to a tree at the edge of the grove, his arms wrapped about the trunk and tied behind him.

"He's secure isn't he," asked Gildersleave.

"I used all the rest of the rope," replied Marsdale.

"Then let him watch," said Gildersleave. "When the

ritual closes and grove burns down to purify itself, he'll burn with it. Unless he finds salvation in watching us, but that's between him and our Lord."

Gildersleave stepped back and assessed the CEO's position of dangling, as though he was evaluating a painting or statue. Satisfied, he walked to the end of the row of bodies and retrieved the ceremonial copper bowl and knife, then he walked back and handed them to the hipster with the man bun who was standing in front of the CEO.

"It's your turn," said Gildersleave. "The ritual closes when the veins of our enemy's leader run dry. Slice away and we can leave."

The hipster with the man bun stroked the tip of the knife with his thumb as he stared at the CEO in contemplation.

As the hipster was working up the nerve to slit the CEO's throat, Mister Lewis was feeling his way around his bonds. It was true, Marsdale probably had used all the rest of their rope, but it seemed artists weren't as good with knots as Viking sailors and it was slowly starting to move. This was escapable for him, although whether it was escapable for his client wasn't entirely up to the knot.

"I'm still not sold on this," said the hipster with the man bun.

"Follow the ritual," said Gildersleave. "It takes eight sacrifices to complete the ritual. You're the one who gets to end this."

The knot was loosening.

"I didn't like dissecting frogs in biology and this is worse," said the hipster with the man bun.

"Don't you want to be debt free," asked Gildersleave.

"Of course," said the hipster with the man bun. "But I believe in my art. It will catch on. I just need to wait on it."

"Fine," growled Gildersleave, "I'll do the cutting myself. Can you at least hold the bowl or are you worried about your precious hands getting splattered?"

"I suppose," acquiesced the hipster with the man bun as he handed Gildersleave the knife.

Gildersleave grabbed the CEO by the hair to steady the head and raised the knife. As he brought the knife down, Mister Lewis shoved Gildersleave's forearm above the knife. The stoke missed the CEO's throat and took a chunk out of Gildersleave's other arm.

Blood spilled from the wound into the copper bowl. There was no clink of gold. Instead, there was a hiss, like water hitting a hot skillet.

"What have you done," whispered Gildersleave, staring in horror at the bowl.

Mister Lewis punched Gildersleave in the face. Gildersleave fell into the hipster with the man bun. The hipster with the man bun dropped the bowl. When the bowl hit the ground, lightning flashed and an image of Loki's face appeared, hovering above the bowl, twice as large as life.

"The rules of the ritual were clear," said Loki's disembodied head. "Eight sacrifices in eight days. Eight sacrifices of those who offend thee, with the final sacrifice being their ruler. You have sacrificed the wrong blood today and it wasn't even a kill. It insults me when you make improper sacrifices. Did you know your Lord of Irony was also the god of wildfire? You shall learn."

The ground around Gildersleave smoldered for a moment before bursting into flame, a flame that quickly spread across Gildersleave's body. His skin darkened and crumbled far quicker than it should have and as it did, the fire spread to the next hipster, repeating the cycle until a minute later when the hipster with the man bun was the only hipster left.

"You shall live to bear witness," Loki's head floated over to hover above the hipster with the man bun and stare down at him. "Tell the others the importance of following the ritual. Independence is neither celebrated nor rewarded."

The image of the head then pivoted to face Mister Lewis.

"I have to admit, unleashing my fire on the bunglers was even more fun than the sacrifices were. This is why I like having you around magician. I'm sure we'll meet again."

And then Loki's head was gone.

"What an asshole," said the hipster in the man bun.

"Of course," replied Mister Lewis. "Loki is the god of the assholes. You just complimented him."

Mister Lewis retrieved the sacrificial knife and cut down the CEO.

"Is it over," asked the CEO.

"Well, that depends what you mean by over," said Mister Lewis. "This group, whatever you call it: cult, coven, cell... it's over. That last one is going to run as far as he can. Loki doesn't have the longest attention span, so that experiment probably died with the cult. Here's the thing, though. That cult didn't exist in a vacuum. Loki may have been manipulating them, but he was really just taking advantage of the situation. He was offering a way out. What you need to be worried about moving forward is that Loki was dealing in ideas. If one catches on, it's much harder to kill an idea than a god."

The CEO stared blankly.

"Come on," sighed Mister Lewis. "Loki's wildfire will burn this grove clean of all traces of his presence. We need to leave."

SURVEILLANCE FROM BEYOND THE VEIL

A Guiding Light

Mister Lewis stared at the pear. It wasn't the first time he'd ever seen a pear hanging from a branch, but it was the first time he'd done so in a building's lobby. Technology companies could be a little flashy, but an orchard in the reception area was a bit much. He moved closer to the orchard's edge and examined a peach tree.

"It's symbolic," said the receptionist, who'd left the front desk and approached.

"I'm not sure I see what symbolism you're going for with the fruit," replied Mister Lewis.

"But there aren't any apples in our orchard. It's a little joke about the competition."

The receptionist led Mister Lewis to the elevator and then to the office of the CEO who had summoned him.

"I hope you live up to your references," said the CEO. "I need to find out what this thing is that's lifting our trade secrets and get rid of it."

"Your description of the anomaly brought to mind some possibilities," Mister Lewis paused as he stepped over a small disc-shaped robot vacuum that was circling the room. "But it's best not to jump to conclusions too quickly."

"Our security is tight and development is compartmentalized," the CEO reddened a bit. "There's something weird going on here and you're supposed to be the expert on weird."

Indeed, Mister Lewis was just such an expert. While his business card read "Physics Consultant," that was merely his sense of humor at work while he established a more publicly palatable front for the true nature of his consulting. Mister Lewis solved problems that defied the laws of physics and were paranormal in nature.

"Is that a custom model," Mister Lewis gestured to the vacuuming robot.

"I don't think so," said the CEO. "Why?"

"Because I don't think those are supposed to have a camera," Mister Lewis picked up the robot and pointed to the telltale glassed off section on its outer curve. "As I understand it, these things have sonar for mapping out the building, too."

The CEO said nothing, but reddened a little more.

"Anything important in that closet," asked Mister Lewis.

"No," said the CEO.

Mister Lewis picked up a trashcan from beside the CEO's desk with his free hand and walked over to the closet. He set the robot down, then turned the trash can upside down over the robot and shut the door.

"That should mess with any microphone a little bit," offered Mister Lewis, "but you'll want to have somebody take that apart. You mentioned you had some video evidence that's not related to spy robots?"

The CEO gestured to a television monitor at the far end of the office and they approached it.

"We've had several witnesses report seeing a strange man with a deformed face," began the CEO. "The man has a very small mouth. Perhaps the size of a penny or a dime. When approached, the man disappears in a flash of light. We have some reports that occurred in front of security cameras."

"Let me guess," interrupted Mister Lewis. "The man doesn't photograph, but the light does?"

"Two days ago," the CEO hit the play button.

The screen showed a mildly crowded hallway. Suddenly all eyes converged on an empty space, then a light flashed in that empty space, almost like a strobe.

"Yesterday," the CEO hit a button on the remote.

A different hallway with only one person in it appeared on the screen. The person's head jerked around in surprise, followed by a burst of light. This time the light didn't blink out right away, rather it faded out as it floated away in the opposite direction of the startled worker.

"And this happened before you arrived today," the CEO hit another button. "That's Mandy Lane, our Chief Information Security Officer.

The screen showed a woman climbing stairs in a stairwell. She stopped in mid-step, eyes widening. The now familiar flash of light hit and she fell over backwards, tumbling down the stairs and out of the camera's focus.

"She OK," asked Mister Lewis.

"Fell down four flights of stairs and got up," said the CEO. "We'll need to talk to her next, but we're not doing it here with that... spybot... in the closet."

Don't Sit Under the Apple Tree

❦

"It's actually here for security," said the CEO, who plucked a peach from a tree and took a bite. "Because this orchard has no electricity inside it, it's easier to sweep for listening devices. At least that's what they told me in the budget meeting."

Mister Lewis and the CEO had retreated to the lobby to meet the Chief Information Security Officer and get her input on the leaks and impressions of the flashes of light.

"And here to make a statement about Apple," said Mister Lewis.

"We'll never let them in here," the CEO nodded and took another bite of the peach.

"You all can come out of there," said the Chief Information Security Officer, who was standing in the lobby outside the orchard, chewing on a stick of beef jerky. "I'm on a no fruit diet, so I'm not going in there."

"Before you fell down the stairs," asked Mister Lewis,

"did you see the same man with a tiny mouth everyone else has reported seeing around the bursts of light?"

"No," said the Chief Information Security Officer. "I just had that light blow up in my face and I fell over. I didn't see anything else."

"We found a camera on a modified vacuuming robot before we came down here," Mister Lewis changed his line of questioning. "It appears that someone in the physical world is definitely trying to spy on you."

"That happens all the time," said the Chief Information Security Officer. "I'll have to look at it."

"What kind of electronic tampering have you seen," asked Mister Lewis. "Process of elimination first."

"You mean intrusions," queried the Chief Information Security Officer. "Nothing that's gotten through. I know my business. There's two places our data sits: on the network and on the screen. It hasn't left either place."

"But information can be observed on-screen, right?"

"We've been sweeping for cameras every day since this all started," growled the Chief Information Security Officer. "There aren't any. And I don't think one of those vacuums could get behind a desk with the right angle to photograph the screen with any consistency. And it would be really obvious if they were trying."

"Oh, I wasn't talking about cameras," said Mister Lewis. "It's much more likely you're haunted and there are ghosts reading over your shoulder."

He'll Eat Anything

✧❦✧

"We're looking for someone with a rice bowl," said Mister Lewis as he, the CEO and the Chief Information Security Officer entered the company cafeteria. "Specifically somebody with a rice bowl who's sitting there and not eating it."

"I'm also on a no rice diet," said the Chief Information Security Officer.

"Is this dangerous," asked the CEO.

"It depends," replied Mister Lewis. "That flash of light your employees are describing is usually indicative of a sort of servant ghost in the East Asian tradition. China, Taiwan. Maybe Japan. Maybe Korea. The type of spirit associated with manifesting those lights was usually obsessed with the corporate ladder before death. They really don't do much except make light. And that small mouthed man, makes it sound like it's also a hungry ghost. What they call a "needle mouth." That's a ghost cursed with a mouth that's too small to eat and is essentially starving, or at least feeling like its starving, while roaming the spirit world. It can't eat you – not with that mouth – so it's mostly harmless. It can, however, be just as annoying in death as the person that came before it likely was in life. The real question is whether this ghost is being directed by a simple spirit medium or we're dealing with a full-on necromancer."

"You mean like Zombies," asked the Chief Information Security Officer, who had traded the beef jerky in for a bag of pork rinds.

"Potentially," said Mister Lewis.

"Zombies are weird," said the Chief Information Security Officer, who then inhaled a handful of pork rinds.

"Could it be the ghost of Steve Jobs," asked the CEO. "Steve Jobs returned from the grave to terrorize the competition?"

"It's too early to rule anything out," replied Mister Lewis. "It seems unlikely, but it depends on what kind of alternative medicine he was into towards the end. Some of those people don't completely understand the forces they're dealing with and there can be... complications. Besides, if it were the ghost of Steve Jobs, there would likely be more shouting and objects flying across the room."

The three of them wandered through the cafeteria, but there were no bowls of rice to be seen.

"Does it have to be a bowl of rice," asked the CEO.

"Not necessarily," replied Mister Lewis. "It needs to be something from the deceased's kitchen, or ancestral kitchen if it's been dead long enough. Something that was commonly eaten. Theoretically, it could be a burrito or a hamburger, if that's what it normally ate when it was human. But a rice bowl is the tradition."

Mister Lewis slowly pivoted in a circle. It did look like everyone in the cafeteria was eating. It didn't mean the medium wasn't there, but the medium didn't have to be hiding in plain sight, either.

"He's eating out of the toilet," came a scream from the edge of the cafeteria.

Mister Lewis and the CEO gave each other puzzled glances and the Chief Information Security Officer kept eating.

A commotion followed the scream as employees exited the bathroom door in a bit of hurry, with looks of disgust setting the tone. Before the door closed, something else exited the bathroom. It looked like a man, but its color was faded like a photograph that had been exposed to sunlight for too long. And if you looked closely, its feet didn't quite touch the ground.

The room got very quiet as the crowd took in the thing that looked like a faded man, and it was a truly strange thing to behold. Its legs shuffled as though it was slowly staggering forward, but floated forward at a rapid clip. The contrast between the motion of the legs and the speed of movement made it even more surreal to watch.

"Where is my cousin," said the faded man in something between a shout and rasp. It then floated over to a trash can and stuck its head in the can. The sounds of chewing were audible all the way in the opposite corner of the cafeteria.

The Chief Information Security Officer took off running in the opposite direction.

"That's about enough of that," a security guard approached the faded man. "What department do you work in? Where's your company ID?"

"Back away from it," yelled Mister Lewis.

The guard ignored him and went to place a hand on the faded man's shoulder. His hand passed straight through it, like trying to grab a rainbow.

The faded man stood up and turned to face the guard. Its jaw lowered, and then kept lowering, stretching out around six inches lower than it should have been able to.

The color drained from the guard's face and a splotch of pulsating light flew from the guard's head into the faded man's mouth. Then the guard collapsed and the faded man clamped its jaw shut.

"Everyone back away," yelled Mister Lewis as he slowly walked over to the faded man.

The faded man re-oriented itself to face Mister Lewis.

"Where is my cousin," it repeated in a howling rasp.

"Yes," replied Mister Lewis. "I'd like to know that, too. It would help if I knew who your cousin was, first."

The faded man scowled at Mister Lewis and again opened its mouth wide. Nothing happened.

"What's the matter," asked Mister Lewis. "My life force is a little harder to eat? I wonder why that is?"

Mister Lewis reached into the breast pocket of his jacket and produced a small red disc at the end of a thin chain.

"Ever seen one of these before," Mister Lewis asked the faded man.

The faded man stared back blankly.

"Not that one, eh," said Mister Lewis, who then fished a blue triangle on a chain out of his left pocket.

The faded man stared blankly.

"Then If I'm still alive," continued Mister Lewis, who reached into his right pocket and produced a green oval on a chain, "it must be this one."

The faded man backed up.

"That's good," said Mister Lewis. "I have extras of that one and I bet they can touch you."

He pulled two more just like it out of his right pocket, clutched the ends of the chains in his hand and swung at the faded man like he was holding a cat-o'-nine-tails.

The faded man screamed.

"Back," Mister Lewis said as he swung again.

The faded man screamed again, but did back up. Mister Lewis kept swinging the chains at it and the faded man kept backing up, letting out a cry of pain anytime one of the green ovals made contact. Mister Lewis backed it down the hallway, into the lobby.

When the faded man got to the orchard in the lobby, it stopped moving. Its head swiveled back and forth between the orchard and Mister Lewis. It looked panicked.

"Yes," said Mister Lewis. "That's what you think it is. Thanks for confirming."

Mister Lewis swung the chains harder and more rapidly, beating the faded man back into the orchard until it backed into the branch of a peach tree. When the branch passed through the faded man's torso, the faded man shimmered and disappeared.

The Family That Plays Together, Stays Together... For Eternity

❧❦❧

"What was that thing," whispered the CEO, who followed Mister Lewis into the orchard.

"That was a different kind of hungry ghost," replied Mister Lewis. "That was a ghost of excessive means. One of the nastier kinds you can meet. It consumes anything cast off by the living. It can also eat the life right out of you if it has a mind to."

"Was that Steve Jobs," asked the CEO. "It was all shout-y."

"Seems unlikely," said Mister Lewis. "But you might want to put this on. Wear it like a necklace."

Mister Lewis handed the CEO one of the green ovals on a chain.

"What is it," asked the CEO.

"That's an amulet," replied Mister Lewis. "Fortunately, you gave me enough detail on the situation before I came over, that I was able to make an educated guess at what was going on. Eliminate some possibilities and bring some toys that might work. That's one of the ones that worked."

The CEO donned the amulet.

"It's something that was used by shamans and priests during exorcisms," continued Mister Lewis. "Keeps the ghost from being able to harm you. Doesn't work on every type of ghost, but it should work on what we've seen so far."

Mister Lewis turned to a peach tree and pulled on a branch until it snapped off.

"Hey," admonished the CEO, "those trees are expensive."

"And worth the money," said Mister Lewis. "Having Steve Jobs on the brain is going to end up making our lives easier. Peach wood is an exorcism tool for this category of ghost. Disrupts their form and dissipates them. You might say your little joke has grown some teeth."

"So Steve Jobs is the cousin it was asking about," asked the CEO.

"Probably not," replied Mister Lewis. "Ancestor worship was common centuries ago and this category of ghost is associated with it. It's unusual for there to be two ghosts in one place unless there was some kind of mass slaughter, though. So far it's looking like both manifestations were subcategories of the hungry ghost class, so it could be related and they could be relatives. Theoretically. This is unnatural, even for a haunting. We need to find out who's summoning them and what the summoner's relationship is to the ghosts and to your corporate secrets. Do you think it more likely it's a rival company or a state actor?"

"Sometimes a government will act on behalf of a company if they think there's enough revenue in it," said the CEO. "There's not always a lot of difference anymore. That robot vacuum with the camera? That's more likely to be a government's resources. These ghosts? I can't even guess if they're related. When you've got something good, everyone tries to get it."

And then someone screamed.

"Do you think your child of light is back," Mister Lewis asked the CEO as he pulled leaves off the peach tree branch and stepped out of the orchard.

The CEO didn't reply, but followed a few steps behind. The two of them entered the hallway connecting the lobby to the rest of the building and found a body with greyish skin lying on the ground, not unlike the security guard in the cafeteria.

"Where is my cousin," came a familiar raspy howl and another faded man turned the corner and floated towards them.

Mister Lewis jabbed at the faded man's face with the peach tree branch. As it happened with the first one, when the branch passed through the faded man, it shimmered and faded into the air.

"It came back," whispered the CEO.

"Worse," said Mister Lewis. "That was another one. Three ghosts in one building. This place isn't built on a cemetery is it?"

"Not that anyone's told me," replied the CEO.

"Either way, that's really not good," said Mister Lewis. "I'd better do a sweep of the building first. Make sure nobody else gets eaten. Just so you know, I start charging extra after the fifth ghost is dispatched."

Possession is 9/10ths of the Law

✿❧❁

The Chief Information Security Officer stopped in mid-chew, froze in her tracks and slowly turned around. Sure enough, there was a faded man floating behind her. It startled her enough she dropped the bag of pork rinds.

"Our cousin," rasped the faded man.

The Chief Information Security Officer backed up a step. The faded man floated forward.

"Our cousin," the faded man repeated.

The faded man's jaw started to lower, only to have the tip of a peach tree branch poke through it. The faded man shimmered and faded out, revealing Mister Lewis holding the branch and the CEO standing behind him.

"Are you alright," asked Mister Lewis.

"Yes," stammered the Chief Information Security Officer.

"You might want to put this on," Mister Lewis reached

into his pocket and produced his last amulet. "It's an amulet that will keep these ghosts off you."

Mister Lewis tossed it to the Chief Information Security Officer, but she let it fall to the floor. The Chief Information Security Officer stared at the amulet for a moment and started running in the opposite direction.

"The supernatural does bring out a fight or flight reaction in a lot of people," Mister Lewis said to the CEO. "And really, flight's usually the safer bet."

"That one said 'our cousin' instead of 'where is my cousin,' didn't it," asked the CEO.

"Correct," said Mister Lewis. "The plural makes it rife with possibilities."

"How many does that make," asked the CEO.

"Eight."

"Is that bad?"

"Nothing about this is good," said Mister Lewis as he picked the amulet off the floor. "We'd better go find her before something else does. That one seemed like it was taking an interest in her."

It took about fifteen minutes to find her. The Chief Information Security Officer had fled to the server room and was folding what looked like origami figures and placing them on a cafeteria tray on top of a desk.

"Paper dolls," asked the CEO.

"Not dolls," said the Chief Information Security Officer, "soldiers."

And the origami did look like men with swords. The Chief Information Security Officer arranged them in a tight circle, as though the paper soldiers were holding hands. Then she dropped a match on the tray the paper soldiers lit up.

"You can't have a fire in the server room," said the exasperated CEO.

The Chief Information Security Officer stared impassively and started to eat a candy bar.

"I should probably handle this," Mister Lewis told the CEO as he pulled him back to the doorway.

The CEO shot him a look, but backed off.

"That chocolate looks good," Mister Lewis said to the Chief Information Security Officer. "You never know how long it will be until the next time you eat."

"Indeed," replied the Chief Information Security Officer, "it could be an eternity before your next meal."

"Isn't it more customary to burn joss money in offering to your ancestors," asked Mister Lewis.

"Joss money takes more time to make," said the Chief Information Security Officer. "I... my ancestors might have more need of soldiers in the afterlife than money. And the need might be urgent."

"She died when she fell down the stairs," asked Mister Lewis.

"It was not my intention," said the Chief Information Security Officer. "It was convenient, however."

"Why do you need an army of soldiers in the afterlife?"

"We are not accustomed to being... directed... as we have been."

"We?"

"My ancestors. My descendants. There are many of us here and the behavior is degrading."

"I can help you with that," Mister Lewis said as he set the peach tree branch on the table. "We're interested in who's making you do this."

"Alas," said the Chief Information Security Officer, "that is a family matter. It should be dealt with from within the family."

"I can't let you stay in there," said Mister Lewis.

"I am not done eating," said the Chief Information Security Officer, who took another bite of the candy bar.

"Too bad," said Mister Lewis as he retrieved the peach tree branch and tossed it into the Chief Information Security Officer's lap.

There was blinding flash of light. The Chief Information Security Officer's head fell sideways to her shoulder, a broken neck no longer being animated. Then her body fell forward onto the desk. Above it floated another sun-faded man, this time bearing a distorted face and the tiniest of mouths.

The needle mouthed faded man glared at Mister Lewis for several seconds. Then it turned and half-walked, half-floated out of the room. Following behind it marched two columns of tiny soldiers, swords aloft, which closely resembled the origami that had been burnt in offering.

"Was that," began the CEO.

"An exorcism," confirmed Mister Lewis. "It couldn't have lasted much longer. Decay would've set in and it would have been obvious. So the bad news is you're down another employee."

"There's good news," asked the CEO.

"As good as you can hope for in a situation like this,"

replied Mister Lewis. "The original ghost took advantage of the situation to reanimate a corpse and make a ritual sacrifice to itself, according to the old customs. It sent soldiers to itself in the afterlife. It's been controlled and it's rebelling against whoever was doing the controlling. We just need to follow it and it will lead us right to whoever is responsible for all this.

A Rice Bowl to Go

❧

The faded man left the building, its procession of soldiers trailing behind it. It went down the building's front steps, took a left at the sidewalk and floated over to a food truck with "Rice After Death" written on its side in bold red letters.

"Finally," yelled the food truck's counter attendant upon looking up. "Where have you been? Do you have any idea how many of our ancestors I've had to summon up and send looking for you?"

Mister Lewis and the CEO left the building's front door and cautiously approached the steps.

"Hiding in plain sight after all," Mister Lewis said to the CEO.

The faded man stared at the counter attendant. It would've frowned, but its needle mouth wasn't wide enough for frowning.

"Come here and report," growled the counter attendant, pulling out an order pad and pen.

The faded man did not move.

"What did you see on their screens," the counter attendant growled louder. "I am ready to transcribe."

Mister Lewis reached the sidewalk.

"Hang back and let me handle this," he said to the CEO.

The counter attendant glared at the faded man and the faded man glared back with eyes that somehow managed to be empty and angry at the same time.

"You want to do this in the traditional manner," the counter attendant reached under the counter and slammed a not very fresh looking bowl of rice on the counter. "There. Rice from our family kitchen. It binds you and I summon you to me."

The faded man struggled to stand still, but floated forward at a slow and jagged pace.

"Report," growled the counter attendant.

The faded man suddenly brought his arm forward and pointed at the counter attendant. The tiny ghost soldiers trailing him surged forward and overran the counter, flipping and pinning the attendants' head to the counter, exposing the throat and pinning the arms down.

The faded man pantomimed a slapping hand and one of the ghost soldiers knocked the rice bowl off the counter. The bowl shattered as it hit cement and the rice spilled all over the sidewalk. The faded man stopped moving towards the food truck.

The faded man repeated the slapping hand motion. A ghost soldier disappeared under the counter and more rice bowls were flung out the counter window. Each time a bowl hit the ground and shattered, another faded man appeared. The faded men all stared at the counter attendant in disgusted judgement.

"You are my ancestors," cried the counter attendant. "You cannot do this to family."

The faded man laughed and it was not a pleasant sound. Then it made a fist and pointed a thumb at its throat.

The ghost soldiers acknowledged the gesture. Two ghost soldiers pulled back on the attendant's chin to better expose the throat and the one that had disposed of the rice bowls raised its tiny sword above its head.

"Hold up a minute," said Mister Lewis, standing two arms' length behind the faded man. "We need to know who your descendent is working with."

The faded man turned its head to face Mister Lewis.

"No," it rasped. "No more."

The ghost soldier brought its blade down on the counter attendant's throat and a flash of light blinded Mister Lewis.

When his vision cleared, the faded men and ghost soldiers had vanished. All that was left was the counter attendant's dead eyes and half severed head hanging out of the food truck's ordering window above an ample amount of blood.

"Where did they go," asked the CEO.

"Back to where they came from," replied Mister Lewis. "Your regular security will have to identify the body. That was the medium we were looking for. Hopefully, they'll be able to trace who the actual client was. Looks like a freelancer to me."

"The ghost turned on the medium," asked the CEO.

"You run a business," said Mister Lewis. "Think of as it a metaphor for mistreating a captive contractor. The worse you mistreat them, the more trouble there is on their way out. It would be best if neither of us were here when the police arrive. I'll send you an invoice for the extra exorcisms."

And then Mister Lewis was gone.

THE SOUL TARIFF

Knock, Knock – What's There?

❦

Mister Lewis felt overdressed. It was a small town and his black suit stuck out like a sore thumb. Everyone was dressed more casually here. In the pharmacy he walked by. In the grocery store. He wondered if the bank tellers dressed down, too, as he passed that building.

Finally, he found what he was looking for. The local funeral home. It looked a little more formal with its classical pillars. It was a bit of a contrast to the rest of the town, except perhaps for the bank. Both were older buildings and Mister Lewis wondered if the slightly more formal architecture was just the sign of a past era for the region.

The door of the funeral home was unlocked, which was usually the case with funeral homes during the day. He entered and found an empty greeting area. Venturing further in, the visitation room was empty. As were the slumber room and the reposing room. Mister Lewis got as far as the arrangement room before he heard the knocking coming from the lower level.

He followed the noise down a set of stairs before it stopped. Following where it had come from, he found himself in the preparation room, giving a quizzical look to a mortician who couldn't stop glancing from side to side at the caskets that filled the room.

"You're Lewis," asked the mortician apprehensively.

"I am," replied Mister Lewis. "You mentioned a problem with the unquiet dead?"

"Just wait for it," said the mortician.

So Mister Lewis waited and, sure enough: two minutes later, the noise began again as coffin lids bounced up and down, with the odd limb protruding and flailing in the air. After it a bit, it all stopped and it was quiet again.

"Regular intervals," asked Mister Lewis.

"Not really," said the mortician. "You never know how long it's going to last, either. Can you do something about it?"

"I can try," said Mister Lewis.

While Mister Lewis had a business card that said "Physics Consultant," that was an inside joke. His real profession was dealing with things that defied the laws of physics and were not natural in origin.

"It's all of them," asked Mister Lewis.

The mortician nodded in affirmation and Mister Lewis approached the nearest coffin. Inside it was a largely intact body that looked prepped for a viewing.

"Has this one been embalmed," asked Mister Lewis.

"They're all been embalmed," said the mortician.

"It's unusual to see possession or reanimation after embalming" Mister Lewis said as he removed a flask out of his inner coat pocket. "The normal solution may work, though."

He splashed the body with water from the flask, placed his hands on the head and muttered under his breath for a minute.

"I don't think that took," said Mister Lewis as he withdrew his hands. "Let's give it a minute."

Three minutes later, the room was filled with the sound of bouncing coffin lids and the body Mister Lewis had laid hands upon was flailing on with the rest of them.

"I'm sorry," said Mister Lewis. "I may have been making some assumptions based on geography. Was the deceased Jewish? That's a slightly different ritual."

The mortician walked over to the coffin, glanced down and said, "Lutheran."

"Lutheran," repeated Mister Lewis. "No, this is not how it normally works at all. Can you tell me how all this started?"

Death and Taxes

✦

"H e said it was a tax matter," said the mortician.

"Who said that," asked Mister Lewis.

"I didn't get his name," replied the mortician. "He was probably in his mid-50s. Long brown beard and a mullet. 5'9" and 250 lbs, but it mostly wasn't muscle. And he dressed in camouflage. He said the souls couldn't leave the mortuary until the excise tax was paid."

"Excise tax," Mister Lewis was perplexed. "Excise tax on what?"

"On the souls. He later called it the Soul Tariff on the souls leaving the body."

"First off, an excise tax and a tariff are two different things," said Mister Lewis.

"I know, but I didn't think he wanted to be corrected."

"Second off," continued Mister Lewis. "While a soul leaving the body and moving to another plane might technically fit into an import/export model for a tariff, nobody does that. Not even in cases of transmigration."

The coffins lids began banging again.

"Who did he say who he was with," asked Mister Lewis.

"He didn't."

Mister Lewis dipped his hand into his right front jacket pocket and produced a monocle. Placing the monocle over his right eye, he approached one of the banging coffins and pulled back the lid.

"And he might not have been lying," Mister Lewis said while squinting through the monocle at the flailing corpse inside the coffin. "There's a soul in there. It belongs to the body, but the body is dead and it hasn't departed. That's not supposed to happen. It's not a possession. It's not a classical re-animation. It's... just there and things are going haywire."

"So he might have really done this," asked the mortician.

"Possibly," replied Mister Lewis. "Something caused it and I've never heard of something precisely like this happening before. I'm not sure if you'd call this extortion or ransom, but it's not taxation any more than a protection racket is insurance. What did this tax collector want for payment?"

"He wanted to be paid in either gold or bags of non-GMO seeds," said the mortician.

"Non-GMO," Mister Lewis paused. "What kind of seeds?"

"Potatoes, corn, tomatoes, squash or amaranth."

"Amaranth..."

"I'm not sure what that is."

"It's more of a South American thing," said Mister

Lewis. "Similar to quinoa, but... never mind. I shouldn't expect this to start making sense. Did this tax collector say where he wanted to collect his tariff?"

"He did," said the mortician. "He said he would be holding office in the old waterbed factory at the edge of town."

"Then I think we should pay him a visit," replied Mister Lewis. "We need to separate out what, if anything, he's actually responsible for and what's just a delusion. He's talking nonsense, but what's happening shouldn't be possible, either."

Taxation Without Rationalization

❧❀❧

The old waterbed factory was more or less in one piece, but it wasn't a pretty sight. The weathered sheet metal building looked like a gigantic shed that had been put up quickly and left to rust in the rain when its utility was over.

Mister Lewis opened the door to the factory. It was essentially a large hall with bits of detritus piled up here and there. The back of the building glowed with a faint orange light. Looking down, Mister Lewis noticed a pair of bear traps on the floor. He motioned to the traps and gave the mortician a quizzical look.

"He did look a bit like a hunter," said the mortician with a shrug.

There were more traps as they moved towards the light at the back of the room. There was no attempt to conceal them, but if you wanted to avoid them altogether, the presence of the traps herded you into a zigzag approach. Eventually, they got to the back and were greeted by an out of shape man with a large, unkempt beard in camouflaged body armor and dilated eyes, who was scowling and holding a shotgun. He was backlit by the orange light and almost looked like he was glowing.

"I'm not seeing any gold or seed bags," said the tax collector.

"And I'm not seeing any taxing authority," said Mister Lewis.

The tax collector paused, twitching a little as he adjusted his flak jacket.

"I am preemptively declaring taxation of the movement of souls as a concerned citizen in advance of the cosmic visitation," declared the tax collector in a voice that was intended to sound authoritative.

"If there was a cosmic visitation, I think I'd know about it," said Mister Lewis.

"Wait," the tax collector said with concern. "Are you from NASA?"

"...maybe."

"Are you the Planetary Protection Officer they hired," asked the tax collector.

"Why," Mister Lewis said in a low and quiet tone.

The tax collector raised his right arm to shoulder level and gestured with his palm upturned. Out from behind him floated an orb of indeterminate material blanketed in an orange glow. It stopped and hovered over his empty hand.

"This arrived ahead of the alien vanguard," said the tax collector.

Mister Lewis did not reply.

"I have to collect the tax before they arrive and collect

it themselves," continued the tax collector. "The aliens invented the soul tariff in ancient Egypt."

"I was not aware of that," said Mister Lewis.

"They hired a Planetary Protector who doesn't watch The Historical Channel," squealed the tax collector in disgust. "And the government wonders why they can't get anything done. This is exactly why patriots like myself have to pick up the reins."

"There probably is a phone call I could make," said Mister Lewis.

"You do that," said the noticeably less friendly tax collector.

Mister Lewis and the mortician zigzagged their way back out of the factory.

Reality Is Open To Interpretation

"That glowing orb is not from outer space," Mister Lewis said to the mortician after they exited the building. "It's an artifact called The Orb of Reslataan. I have no idea what it's doing out here, but you'd be surprised how often mystic artifacts go missing and turn up in unexpected places."

"That's what's holding my bodies hostage," asked the mortician.

"Maybe," replied Mister Lewis. "But it's supposed to be used to communicate with the dead and potentially trap a soul within it, but not bind them to their mortal shells. Did this begin before he turned up?"

"Sort of," said the mortician. "It began about 5 minutes before he walked in the door and demanded I pay taxes on their souls."

"Then the orb probably has something to do with it," mused Mister Lewis.

"Why does he think it's from aliens," asked the mortician.

"It sounds like he's watched too many conspiracy shows on cable television," offered Mister Lewis. "Although I suppose it's possible that's also why this is happening. If he thinks it came from ancient astronauts who visited Egypt, then he's clearly not trained on how to use it. It's entirely possible he doesn't understand how it's working and... you know how any sufficiently advanced technology would be indistinguishable from magic? He's assumed that magic is a sufficiently advanced technology."

A scream came from behind the pair, followed by a crash. They turned around to see a car with blood on the hood and a broken body lying on the ground several feet away. The body lay still, and then its limbs started flailing. A minute later it was still again.

"The effect isn't confined to your mortuary," said Mister Lewis. "If that's a field that's leaking outward, it's hard to tell what's going on and how exactly to shut it off. For all we know, the Orb could be damaged and it may not be as simple as turning it off."

"Do you know how to shut it off if it isn't broken," asked the mortician.

"I know how to use that type of an artifact," said Mister Lewis. "Shutting down a non-standard use, if that's what it is? I'd need to try it to find out. Regardless we need to get that thing away from him before more damage is done, permanent or not. If he's got an active enough imagination, maybe I can talk our way out of this."

Zero Sum Negotiation

❧❧❧

Mister Lewis and the mortician zigzagged their way back through the warehouse to where the tax collector still stood.

"We're prepared to make you an offer," said Mister Lewis.

"We," asked the tax collector.

"I am wearing a black suit, aren't I," replied Mister Lewis.

The tax collector stared at Mister Lewis, his hand fumbling in his pocket until it produced a pill bottle. The tax collector popped the top off the bottle, fished out the last pill and swallowed it as he tossed the bottle to the floor.

"What kind of an offer," asked the tax collector.

"We'll pay for the orb," replied Mister Lewis.

"I can't do that," the tax collector said, while jerking slightly as though something was running up and down his spine. "That belongs to the aliens, not some government types who don't officially exist."

"The aliens," said Mister Lewis. "Which aliens are they exactly? What's their name?"

"The aliens," said the tax collector, "are just the aliens. They're not into fancy names or titles, like you are, 'Planetary Protector.' What you need to do is pay up before the aliens notice I put the soul traffic on pause."

"What do aliens care about human souls leaving their bodies," asked Mister Lewis with a frown.

"Damn, but you NASA boys are ignorant," howled the tax collector. "Just look up. The chemtrails in the sky are the highway that souls travel on to join the aliens."

"I suppose that was on the Historical Channel, too," sighed Mister Lewis.

"Of course not," grunted the tax collector. "Those videos are on the Internet. You need to widen your horizons."

The discarded pill bottle rolled to a stop against the mortician's shoe, who then picked it up and pocketed it.

"And you aren't concerned about upsetting the aliens by disrupting their soul harvest," Mister Lewis fished.

"Don't you know anything about logic," the tax collector reddened and paused to collect himself. "Let me spell this out for you, nice and simple. You're going to pay me to let the souls go. Then I'm going to use the money to bribe the U.N. not to seize my farm with eminent domain. The United Nations is a front for the aliens and after they communicate back to their masters about how efficient I am, the aliens will reward me for my initiative and make me their viceroy on Earth. And it I'm lucky, they'll also reward me with some of their fine alien women. It's the American Dream!"

"Yes," said Mister Lewis, struggling to maintain a neutral look on his face. "That's very... logical."

"You're terrible at your job," shouted the tax collector. "You need to get on the Internet and learn how the world works, not how the corrupt media and lying science books want you to think it works."

"Start heading for the door," Mister Lewis hissed to the mortician, who began backing away.

Mister Lewis turned back to face the tax collector.

"That's one option," he said, "but there's another option I like better. Something about nine-tenths of the law."

Mister Lewis raised his arm, palm facing towards the tax collector and cupped his fingers. The glowing orb slowly floated up and out from behind the tax collector and kept moving in the direction of Mister Lewis.

"How in the hell," the tax collector's voice trailed off and he dropped his shotgun in shock. He glared at the orb, face turning red in a cocktail of anger and concentration. The orb slowed and then stopped.

"Oh. Shit."

Mister Lewis swore and started running for the exit when orb stopped moving. He was doing a fair approximation of the triple jump, hopping over clusters of bear traps when the orb returned to the tax collector's hand and the tax collector dove for his shotgun.

"You can't steal what's mine," screamed the tax

collector as he squeezed the trigger, but he'd taken too long picking up the gun.

As he hit the street, Mister Lewis could hear traps snapping shut, triggered by the buckshot bouncing around the old factory.

Waiting for a Funeral

The mortician was looking out the front window of his mortuary.

"I don't see anything yet," said the mortician.

"Oh, he's coming," replied Mister Lewis. "He's pissed and he doesn't have his gold. Let him come. You got a good look at him. I wouldn't say he's exactly tweaking, but he's overly wired and twitchy. Something's not right with him and I'm betting the excitement and running around wears him out."

"I think he's supposed to be wired," the mortician tossed Mister Lewis the pill bottle retrieved from the factory. "This is what he's taking."

The label said "Raging Wood" in bold red letters. The ingredients were largely caffeine and pseudo-ephedrine.

"Is this supposed to be a natural male enhancement pill," asked Mister Lewis.

"I think he probably saw it on one of those Internet

videos he was going on about," said the mortician. "I don't think it would work, though."

"No way it could give him 'Raging Wood,'" said Mister Lewis. "It might even have the opposite effect. That's a banned bodybuilding supplement, if I recall correctly. But it will absolutely make him crash when it leaves his system if he's popping them frequently. We'll just wait him out and jump him when he's woozy. Hopefully, no permanent damage has been done by then."

He was interrupted by a crashing noise from the basement.

"That didn't sound like coffin lids," said the mortician.

The mortician headed towards the basement door with Mister Lewis close behind. Behind the door, shakily climbing the stairs, was a what almost looked like a conga line of dead bodies.

"Were they supposed to be able to walk," asked the mortician as the first corpse in the line snapped its teeth. "And can you shut them off?"

"It didn't work before," said Mister Lewis, "So it's not going to work now. And the laying of hands on one isn't safe if they're moving like that."

"I learned a new trick," came the tax collector's voice over a bullhorn, which sounded like it was near the front door. "Do you think I can make them eat you? Pay your tariff!"

It's Better to Be Lucky than Good

The first corpse was nearing the top of the stairs, its teeth still snapping. Mister Lewis descended one step, put his foot in the corpse's chest and kicked off. It fell backwards, collapsing the line behind it and the row of bodies fell down the stairs. The pile they made writhed as the half-coordinated things tried to untangle themselves and stand.

"We need to block this," said Mister Lewis, pointing to a display cabinet which he and the mortician proceeded to drag in front of the door, followed by a desk and a couple of large chairs.

"The bodies," began the mortician. "Are they zombies now?"

"Not really," replied Mister Lewis. "It's not really clear what they are and there may not be a name. It's probably something between a wight and a zombie. The soul is still present in the body, but it doesn't appear to be in control. It's... an unconventional existence, even contrasted with the spectrum of reanimation."

"Are they strong enough to open the door?"

"Just one? Probably not. The whole group? Unfortunately, we're just going to have to find out."

The sound of clacking teeth distracted them and another animated corpse stumbled in through the hallway door.

Mister Lewis kicked at the side of its right knee and its leg caved. He repeated the process with the left leg and then, as it tried to flail, stomped on the arms until cracking sounds were heard and the flailing was minimal and more of a flopping motion. Then rolled it against the wall with a series of kicks and pinned it there with a heavy sofa. The sofa bounced ever so slightly, but stayed in place.

"Does it feel pain," asked the mortician.

"It's more a question of what's there to feel the pain," explained Mister Lewis. "The soul may still be in the vessel, but it shouldn't be wired up to the nervous system at this point. If the pain receptors are still working, it's a question of whether there's part of a human still driving the body. No human left, then nothing left to feel the pain. Either way, if I can't exorcise them and they're already dead, the only thing we have left is to immobilize and contain them. They can't bite what they can't reach."

"Hey," came the tax collector's voice through the bullhorn. "You mind telling me if those bodies swallow after they take a bite out of you? I didn't really think about that before I gave them orders and I'm not sure how it's gonna work."

The mortician gave Mister Lewis a concerned glance, who shrugged in reply.

"I know you're not dead," continued the tax collector. "I'd be informed of that. So since you're not, do you think we could hurry this thing along and you could pay the tariff? The sooner I can present my tribute, the sooner I get to meet the ladies."

"And this orb is how he's doing this," asked the mortician.

"It must be," replied Mister Lewis. "But this is unknown territory. He must have somehow bonded with the orb and unlocked a previously undiscovered toolset. A lot of discoveries are accidental. Teflon was an accident. Penicillin was an accident. If he thinks this is all the work of aliens, he has no idea why this is really happening, and his grasp on the how of it is probably tenuous. But it's happening, and the means we're going to have to deal with it."

A tapping could be heard on the far side of the basement door.

"If there's probably not a human intelligence inside those things," asked the mortician, "are they likely to be aware enough of their surroundings to find the back stairs?"

Ready for Love

The back stairs secured, they returned to the front room of the mortuary. The tapping on the door to the front stairs was now pounding, though the furniture barricade was still holding.

Then pounding started to come from the front door, as well. Peering through the window, they discovered another animated corpse trying to get in.

"Your basement doesn't have an outside exit," asked Mister Lewis.

"No," said the mortician. "It must've died outside. That's a problem, isn't it?"

"Depends how many people die," said Mister Lewis. "One or two won't make a difference, but we've got a problem if we get swarmed. If he's controlling a wide enough area, this could get ugly fairly quickly."

"And we just have to wait until his concentration lapses?"

"Unless you can tell me how to conjure up a heart attack, yeah."

They gazed into the street and the tax collector stood in the middle of the street, shotgun in hand and orb floating over his shoulder. His head bobbed a bit, then he produced a pill bottle and swallowed a pill.

"He's going to be awake a long time if he keeps popping caffeine pills," observed the mortician.

"Let me see that bottle again," said Mister Lewis.

The mortician handed him the empty bottle of Raging Wood and he looked at the ingredient list again.

"Yes, popping these frequently would explain why he almost looks like he's tweaking," said Mister Lewis. "They're strong and he's doing his own dosage. And he's probably wondering why they're not making loins stir."

"The power of branding," offered the mortician.

"It gives me something to work with," said Mister Lewis. "As long as he still thinks I work for NASA. We need to make his delusions work for us instead of trying to understand them. You can't reason with a nut, but you can push them in the right direction."

He walked over to the window and opened it.

"You win," Mister Lewis yelled as he stuck his head out the window.

"You ready to pay," the tax collector spoke into his bullhorn.

"Better," Mister Lewis shouted back. "Nobody knows this, but NASA is working with the aliens."

"I knew it," came the tax collector's agitated reply. "That's why you leave the chemtrails alone."

"Look," Mister Lewis continued. "My partner's in

here. She's one of the alien women. I want to send her out, but..."

"Send her out!"

"Slow down. She wants to reward you and she's ready to go. Which means you need to be ready to go. Immediately. She's not patient. Are you following me?"

The tax collector froze up, then glanced down at his crotch.

"You just give me a minute," said the tax collector with a hint of anxiety.

The tax collector retrieved his pill bottle, put it to his lips and started swallowing.

"I'm going to collect myself now," the tax collector said, failing to be inconspicuous about glancing down.

They waited.

The tax collector's expression became gradually more concerned as he stood there. He grew red. He twitched a little. Then he convulsed and faceplanted in the middle of the street.

A moment later there was a thud as the corpse at the front door collapsed and crash came from the stairs as though several things had fallen down it.

Mister Lewis moved the sofa back from the wall an inch to check on the corpse there. It was still.

"I think we're clear," said Mister Lewis. "Whatever his connection was to those animated bodies must've severed when he dropped. And we're lucky. If that didn't stop it, I'm not sure if I'd be able to figure out exactly what he was doing in order to reverse the processes."

"And I suppose he's not the first out of shape weekend

warrior to overdose on a workout supplement," added the mortician.

"You'd be in a position to know."

"Yes, I would."

Mister Lewis opened the door and stuck out his arm. The orb flew to his hand.

"Now why did you do all that," Mister Lewis asked the orb.

It didn't reply, it just silently glowed.

"There are too many eternal mysteries in this business, but I think there's something I could use you for," said Mister Lewis as he put the orb in his coat pocket and walked over to the still body of the tax collector.

"You had some natural talent for magic. If you didn't believe everything you saw on the Internet, you would have been dangerous."

TERM LIMITS DON'T
MATTER IF YOU HAVE
ENOUGH CHILDREN

You Can't Have a Secret Past If You Don't Have a Past

❧❧❧

The state capital was a quiet enough small city, as was often the case with state capitals. If there was too much to do, more politicians would get themselves in trouble. Enough got themselves in trouble without there being much to do.

Mister Lewis entered the office of the State Board of Elections and was immediately greeted by the Deputy Director.

"You're Lewis," asked the Deputy Director.

"I'm Lewis," said Mister Lewis.

"Good," said the Deputy Director. "We've got a mess we need cleared up fast and you came up as quick and discrete."

"We should talk about that," said Mister Lewis. "I didn't get a full description of the assignment and I don't usually get involved in elections."

The Deputy Director glanced over both shoulders

nervously and beckoned Mister Lewis to an office in the back of the suite.

"One of the things we do here," began the Deputy Director, "is register candidates. Confirm certain details about them. Eligibility, residence, background... that sort of thing. We've got a candidate for governor that we just can't find any records for. No birth certificate. No tax records. No driver's license. It's like he doesn't exist."

"That doesn't really sound like something you need a physics consultant for," replied Mister Lewis. His business card read "Physics Consultant," but that was something of an in-joke. Mister Lewis consulted on things that went bump in the night, howled at the moon and defied the laws of physics.

"Normally it wouldn't," conceded the Deputy Director. "But this one isn't going by the book. Every time I send someone over to the candidate's campaign office to inquire about the irregularities, they come back telling me that everything is fine and no paperwork is needed. We should just put the candidate right on the ballot and not give it a second thought. It's not natural."

"Ah," said Mister Lewis. "A couple of possibilities spring to mind, although this is a bit unusual for the territory. When do you need to have this candidate vetted or bounced by?"

"Normally," said the Deputy Director, "we'd have a least a month before sending the sample ballots out for printing. The thing is, this candidate is leading in the polls. I'm not sure how long we can hide the questions about official status. It's already an embarrassment if there's something wrong and it's only going to get worse the longer it takes. We have to work quickly."

"Are you the final authority on who goes on the ballots," asked Mister Lewis.

"Yes," answered the Deputy Director.

"And have you met with the candidate directly about this or the candidate's staff?"

"That's supposed to happen in three days. I'd like to know what's going on before then."

"If you actually have that meeting, there's a good chance you won't remember that there was anything going on and simply place the name on the ballot."

The Deputy Director thought for a moment.

"However we need to do it," sighed the Deputy Director, "let's just do it quickly so I can deal with the fallout."

"If it comes to it," offered Mister Lewis, "my services can be extended to include providing a rational-sounding explanation for the events."

"Rational," the Deputy Director was startled. "If something rational happened in politics around here, people would be suspicious."

Working a Crowd

✦❧✦

I t isn't hard to find a candidate in an election year. Stake yourself out in a coffee shop or diner and one is bound to amble through before too long. And it was in a diner that Mister Lewis found the Gubernatorial Candidate.

"That's how you work a room," the Deputy Director pointed at the Gubernatorial Candidate shaking hands with whoever presented themselves. "Pure artistry in pressing the flesh."

"Isn't hand shaking fairly standard," asked Mister Lewis.

"Not like that," replied the Deputy Director. "There's finesse. Just look."

Mister Lewis looked at the candidate and then back to the Deputy Director.

"I think you should probably wait outside," he said to the Deputy Director. "I can't tell if you're just giddy or you're particularly sensitive to something. Some people are more easily influenced than others."

The Deputy Director left with a frown and Mister Lewis positioned himself in the Gubernatorial Candidate's path with hand extended.

"And how are you," asked the Gubernatorial Candidate, showing way too many teeth that were entirely too white and sparkly.

"I'm great," said Mister Lewis. "But I need to ask you a couple questions."

"That's what campaigns are for," said the Gubernatorial Candidate with a bit more pep than was absolutely necessary.

"Where were you born," asked Mister Lewis.

"Oh, that's not really an important issue," said the Gubernatorial Candidate. "But increasing school funding while cutting both the personal and corporate tax rates is."

"Not really my issue," said Mister Lewis. "But I would be curious which township you've been living in and how long?"

"Minor details," the Gubernatorial Candidate was still shaking hands with Mister Lewis and squeezed a bit tighter while locking eyes with him. The Gubernatorial Candidate's eye twinkled, changing color in a pulsing rhythm, following the cadence of the words being spoken. "But you're not really concerned with anything other than voting for me, are you?"

"Sorry," replied Mister Lewis. "I'm from out of state. I don't vote here."

The Gubernatorial Candidate abruptly dropped the

handshake, mouth agape. Before the Gubernatorial Candidate could regain composure, a large fly appeared and started circling the Gubernatorial Candidate, making a particularly loud buzz while doing so.

"I must get to my next appearance," the Gubernatorial Candidate said in a burst and then bolted towards the nearest door.

The fly buzzed around Mister Lewis for a couple seconds and it too went away.

"The Gubernatorial Candidate tried to charm me for my vote," Mister Lewis said to the Deputy Director when he went outside.

"All candidates try to charm you for your vote," said the Deputy Director. "It's in the job description, but not all of them are any good at it."

"Not that kind of charm," replied Mister Lewis. "Charm as in mystical brainwashing to do the caster's bidding. In this case, dictating who to vote for. You've got a ringer running for Governor."

Spreading Joy and Cheer

❧

"We've got a couple more."

Back in the Deputy Director's office, a nervous clerk stuck a head in.

"A couple more what," growled the Deputy Director.

"Two more candidates with no verifiable personal history or details," offered the clerk.

"When did they file," asked the Deputy Director.

"This week," said the clerk. "A lot of people filed this week."

"What are they running for," asked the Deputy Director.

"One for state Senate, one for state House of Representatives," said the clerk.

"Do the districts overlap," interjected Mister Lewis.

"No," said the clerk. "One's on the north side of the state and the other's near the southern border."

"Are they both running for the same political party," asked Mister Lewis.

"No," said the clerk, consulting a piece of paper.

"Out of all the people who've turned in candidate paperwork this week, how many have you been able to vet so far," asked Mister Lewis.

"One out of thirty-four," the clerk stared at the floor.

"You're not suggesting," the Deputy Director's eyebrow rose involuntarily.

"It's a mistake to rule anything out prematurely," Mister Lewis replied. "But, it could be an infestation."

Flies and Lying on the Campaign Trail

❧❀❧

The Candidate for State Senate sat in a chair sipping lemonade and listening keenly to senior citizens voice a variety of opinions on the general state of affairs of the world. The coffee shop catered to an older crowd and Mister Lewis was immediately a conspicuous face.

Reaching into his coat pocket, Mister Lewis palmed a small mirror and arranged himself to get a view of the Candidate for State Senate in that mirror. The Candidate for State Senate's appearance was the same in the mirror as it was to the naked eye, but there was something about those eyes, pulsating with a slight change of color while chatting up voters. Another charmer.

Mister Lewis left the mirror in his palm and worked his way to position himself between the candidate and the entrance. As he stood there, a swarm of five or six flies swept into the room and made sport of buzzing around the head of Mister Lewis, which caused him to swipe his hand in the air to brush them away.

The commotion of scattering the flies drew a sour look from the Candidate for State Senate, who made an excuse that there was an appointment that had to be kept and made for the door around the opposite edge of the room.

Mister Lewis slid over to block the exit.

"Are you one of my supporters," asked the Candidate for State Senate, unable to get around Mister Lewis.

"I just had a question for you," said Mister Lewis, glancing down at the mirror in his palm and noticing no change in appearance up close. "What's your position on strengthening the residency requirements for public office and increasing financial disclosure for candidates."

The Candidate for State Senate smiled broadly, a time-honored delaying tactic for that profession and an opportunity for the questioner to fill in the silence with a different question. Mister Lewis opted to continue the silence, only to have the silence broken by more buzzing from the return of the flies.

"Do we know each other," came a voice from behind Mister Lewis.

He turned around to find a woman who looked to be near the end of her pregnancy staring at him with a peculiar grin on her face.

"I'm just sure that we've met before," said the woman, with the hint of a knowing giggle in her voice.

"I'm not sure that we have," said Mister Lewis. "But you must excuse me, I was talking to the..."

He turned his head back to the Candidate for State

Senate. The Candidate for State Senate was no longer there. He turned his head back to the pregnant woman and she, too, had vanished.

He pivoted his head around the room. Neither was still in the coffee shop.

He stepped outside. Neither was anywhere on the street. They had simply vanished.

The flies hadn't vanished, though. They continued to buzz around his head.

Multiplication Isn't Just For Rabbits

❦

"I t's not an illusion," Mister Lewis was back at the State Board of Elections, reporting to the Deputy Director. "If it were an illusion, I'd have seen a different image in the mirror."

"So that's what the Candidate for State Senate really looks like," asked the Deputy Director. "We're a talking a human being, just maybe one that knows hypnosis?"

"Not necessarily," replied Mister Lewis. "I said it wasn't an illusion. There are things out there that change their form. Physically change it. That's not an illusion and the mirror will still show that altered physical form."

"You mean like werewolves?"

"That's probably not what's happening here, but yes. Lycanthropy is one example of an actual physical change of appearance. Incidentally, we're not dealing with hypnosis here. It's magically induced compulsion. Different thing entirely."

They were interrupted by the return of the nervous clerk.

"More bad news," said the clerk.

"Now what," groaned the Deputy Director.

"Five more candidates don't check out," said the clerk.

"Overlapping districts," asked Mister Lewis.

"Nope," said the clerk. "And not all in the same party, either. All over the state."

"This is starting to sound like an infestation, at a minimum," mused Mister Lewis.

"Is this the Russians," asked the Deputy Director. "Hacking the voter database wasn't enough, so now they're hacking the candidates?"

"You'd think the Russians would be more interested in Federal offices," said Mister Lewis. "But you wouldn't want to rule out anything prematurely."

Representative to a House of Political Repute

❧

Mister Lewis first found the Candidate for State Representative at the editorial offices of the state capital's newspaper, but it didn't seem like a particularly discrete place to ask questions. He waited and followed and soon enough, the Candidate for State Representative entered yet another diner to canvas the local voters.

Mister Lewis took a good look around this diner when he entered. It was only half full with what looked to be a middle class crowd. Thankfully, there didn't appear to be any flies in this one. He waited until the Candidate for State Representative had gotten to the back corner before closing in. Sometimes cornering a candidate is a literal thing.

"And what's your name," asked the Candidate for State Representative, turning away from the booth and finding Mister Lewis standing there.

"Names aren't really important," replied Mister Lewis. "I did have a couple questions, though."

"I don't know," said the Candidate for State Representative. "There's power in names if you know what to do with them. Ask away."

"I was wanting to get your opinion on your opponent's eligibility to run," Mister Lewis lied. "There's a rumor going around he doesn't really live in the district. How do you feel about these districting laws?"

"It's very important to make sure the boundaries of a district conform to demographic concentrations of the will of the people and leave flexibility for the geometry of borders," replied the Candidate for State Representative. "Residency is a state of mind."

"Could you comment on your investments in fossil fuels," Mister Lewis asked, not even trying to look for meaning in the answer's word soup. "Your financial disclosure form indicated a lot of money tucked away there."

"My financial disclosure form?"

"Yes, the one that every candidate files as part of the eligibility process. The state posts them online now. It's new."

Mister Lewis wondered what the reaction would be to hearing that a form that purposefully wasn't filed had appeared online for all to see. Denial of the report? Denial that a necessary piece of paperwork had been filed? With his quarry already physically in a corner, ducking out would be difficult here.

The immediate reaction was a confused look and a

pause. Then, the Candidate for State Representative's eyes started pulsing. The most predictable response of all.

"Personal investments are a private matter," said the Candidate for State Representative in a soothing voice. "You should tell all your friends that and encourage them to look more towards the values of a candidate. You should tell them I have excellent values."

"I must just have a filter for some things," Mister Lewis smirked, but was could only get half his thought out before being cut off.

"We do meet everywhere, don't we," came a familiar voice from behind him.

He turned his head to see the same pregnant woman who disappeared from the coffee shop. This time he quickly took a step back to get both of them in front of him.

"We do," agreed Mister Lewis. "I'm afraid I never got your name, though."

"I thought you didn't like names," said the Candidate for State Representative.

"He knows my name very well," said the pregnant woman. "I'm sure he carries it in his heart."

"I'm sure it's a bewitching name," snorted Mister Lewis.

"Hardly anything so mundane," replied the pregnant woman. "You know I'm much more than that."

As Mister Lewis opened his mouth to respond, the lights flickered and went out for a moment. When they came back on, there was no one in front of him. He spun around, but he didn't actually need to look to know they were gone. They couldn't have physically gotten past him without making contact. Not by mortal means, at least.

Invasion of Vote Snatchers

❧

"The number is eighteen," said the nervous clerk, who was now sweating visibly.

"Eighteen out of thirty-four candidates to register this week don't have any paper trail," asked the Deputy Director. "No evidence they exist. Do I have that right?"

"That's correct," said the clerk.

"Is this some kind of takeover attempt," the Deputy Director addressed his question to Mister Lewis. "Throw a bunch of... I don't know... sleeper agents into the statehouse and then do... something?"

"It's possible not all eighteen are part of this," said Mister Lewis, "but it certainly has the appearance of an organized incursion."

"We should start disqualifying people," the Deputy Director paused as a large fly buzzed into his office and circled over his head.

"Not if you want to find out who or what is behind this," said Mister Lewis.

"They already seem to know you're onto them," the Deputy Director swatted at the fly with a rolled up piece of paper. "Maybe it's time we called the Feds in on this. This could be bad."

"They seem to know me, but they don't necessarily know I'm working for the Board of Elections," said Mister Lewis, eyeing the fly. "The plan likely isn't blown until they're not on the ballot. Until then... what is it with flies in this town?"

Mister Lewis snatched the fly out of the air and squeezed his fist around it. It did not go as planned. Instead of a tiny squish, it felt more like crushing a peanut shell. Then there was the blood. Blood squirted out between his fingers much like juice would squirt out if he were squeezing an orange.

He unclenched his fist and let the contents drop the table. Lots of blood and the body of a fly. The fly was still moving. No, moving wasn't quite the right word. The fly's head was throbbing. Growing. And taking on a more human aspect as it grew.

The head stopped growing when it reached the size of a thumbnail, then Mister Lewis wiped the blood off the head. He knew that face.

"Am I mistaken," Mister Lewis asked the Deputy Director, "or is that the face of your poll-leading Gubernatorial Candidate?"

The Deputy Director, shocked silent, nodded in agreement.

"No Feds," said Mister Lewis. "I know what we're dealing with now. Incidentally, this consultation is now on the house. I'll be settling a different tab when I make my next stop."

Father's Office

N one of the Gubernatorial Candidate's staff seemed to recognize Mister Lewis when he strode into campaign headquarters. He wasn't sure whether that surprised him or not. It was entirely possible most or none of the staff didn't know what was employing them.

Eventually a campaign worker approached him.

"I'm sorry," said the worker. "Our candidate isn't here right now."

"Did your candidate indicate when guests would be received," asked Mister Lewis with sardonic undertones to his voice.

"We're not entirely sure where our candidate is, to be honest."

"Well, that I can clear up for you," said Mister Lewis. "Your candidate went on a fact finding mission. It didn't go well."

The buzzing of flies was heard in the background and

Mister Lewis saw a swarm of twenty or so flying in from the back of the building.

"I don't think your candidate will be coming back," Mister Lewis said in a louder voice.

"What are you talking about," asked the campaign worker.

"But that's all OK," Mister Lewis said, staring at the hovering flies. "I really came to meet with the candidate's father."

"I haven't met the candidate's father," said the befuddled worker. And then the worker froze in place.

"Is there something you want," the pregnant woman was suddenly standing in the middle of the files.

Mister Lewis glanced around the headquarters. The entire staff was frozen still. Only he, the pregnant woman and the flies were moving.

"Fewer games," Mister Lewis stepped forward to stare the woman in the eyes. "I'm here to see the father."

"Some of us are quite fond of games," said the pregnant woman.

"Fine," replied Mister Lewis. "Then let's thin the herd."

His arm shot out and his hand closed around a fly. Once more blood squirted from between his fingers and dripped onto the floor.

When he looked back up, the woman was still pregnant, but her face had changed. Now she had long flowing red hair and an equally long and much thicker red beard. Flames danced above her eyes instead of eyebrows. Her head was that of Loki, god of tricksters, god of wildfire and the last survivor of Asgard.

"Have you caught up with the game yet, magician," asked Loki. "Hold on for a moment. I was planning on taking this one to full term, but it's close enough. We'll talk after the birth."

Loki gritted his teeth, grunted and an extremely large and lumpy baby hit the ground and rolled out from under his maternity dress.

Make Your Own Village to Raise Your Children

❧❀❧

"Carrying your own children again," asked Mister Lewis.

"Sometimes the old ways are the best," said Loki with a smile bigger than his political offspring. "Never underestimate a mother's bond with her children. Yes, we gods can have it both ways. It hurts every time, too. You'd think a being like me would be above that, but even the gods sometimes answer to nature."

Loki's body shifted back to a male form and his preferred skinny jeans and fur coat ensemble. He leaned over the baby on the ground. It was already the size of a three-year-old and rapidly growing.

"This one could grow up to be president," he said. "But I suppose I'll need a new governor first. You shouldn't have been able to kill the last one, but their bodies do grow faster than their brains."

The baby was now the size of an eight-year-old. Loki grabbed its chin and forced eye contact.

"Look at me, child."

The baby grew faster and after 10 seconds it was the very image of the Gubernatorial Candidate.

"They grow up so quickly," said Loki.

"Since you've been down the motherhood road before," Mister Lewis asked, "who was the father this time? Another horse?"

Loki glared at Mister Lewis, the flames of his eyebrows almost jumping off his face.

"Would you be more disturbed imagining your own truth or knowing the real thing," Loki returned the question. "Why don't we say I've cleaned up my bloodlines and leave it at that. You've been very slow answering your own questions this time, magician. Is not taking the form of a fly to bedevil my adversaries a famous part of the oral tradition the mortals paid tribute to me with?"

"I'm supposed to spend my time studying your myths," Mister Lewis was incredulous. "I'm not your monk and I think we established at our last meeting that you weren't an active religion anymore. I figured out the flies and I know about your shapeshifting motherhood going back to pre-history, so let's get on with it."

"Yes, let's," Loki snapped his fingers. "Children?"

The swarm of flies took a human form. No, that wasn't quite right. These were giants, not humans and they all stood around eight feet tall. Even so, Mister Lewis recognized several of them as the phantom political candidates he had been hired to investigate. The giants formed a semi-circle behind their father/mother and boxed Mister Lewis in.

"So now you want to run a state," said Mister Lewis. "How bored are you?"

"Run a state," scoffed Loki. "Where would be the fun in that? No, I want to break a state and see how broken I can make it before those fool mortals can grasp what's happened to them. And if they do recognize what's happening to them, do you think they'll be capable of doing anything but blaming the other party? That won't do much good. I'll have my children running both sides of this nebulous political fence. I'm going to line everyone up like so many sheep and herd them right over a financial cliff. Then I'll eat popcorn while their broken bodies try to crawl out of the wreckage. And maybe, just maybe I'll tease them and grant them the term limits they keep asking for. It would only be an illusion. My children can change form and run again. Or I can have more children. Term limits don't matter if you have enough children, and I'll vote them in, too."

Loki was the god of tricksters, but he was also the god of assholes.

"But why are you here, magician," Loki asked. "Why are you trying to kill my very replaceable children?"

"It's a debt."

"Really," Loki was incredulous. "I thought you made your money following me around and trying to spoil my fun?"

"Except for the time you killed my client before he could pay me," explained Mister Lewis with a certain amount of bitterness. "I tend to remember things like that."

"Ahhh," Loki exhaled. "You're mixing blood debts

with finance. Now I understand. Why Mister Lewis, that is a very Viking attitude you've adopted. It makes an old god happy to see his teachings survive after all these centuries. Unfortunately, I'm going to have to burn that out of you."

"So you're still the god of wildfire," Mister Lewis had more sarcasm in his tones than was strictly necessary.

"Where the lightning strikes the leaves, so was I born," the flames of Loki's eyebrows danced higher as he spoke and murder glinted in his eyes. "God of wildfire, god of manipulation, god of the backdoor."

Mister Lewis smiled back at him and dipped his hand into a coat pocket, producing a small, round snow globe. He made a show of shaking it up and staring at it.

"As a god of Vikings, do you still like the snow?"

He tossed the globe to Loki, who caught it and peered into it.

"Snow," said Loki. "I see only water."

"Exactly," said Mister Lewis.

Loki tried to toss the globe aside, but it was stuck to his hand. When he looked closer, he realized his hand was being pulled into the globe, which was now emitting an orange light.

"What have you done," gasped Loki.

"Just an old orb I came across in my travels," replied Mister Lewis, grinning as Loki's arm was sucked into the globe. "I was saving it for you. Yes, I filled it with water. I wonder... can a god of wildfire become a drowned god?"

Loki's shoulders and head were pulled into the globe next. Then his torso. And finally, his feet.

When Mister Lewis bent over to pick up the globe, he saw a tiny Loki inside it, banging his fists on the walls.

"I wonder if I learned anything besides blood debt from the god of tricksters," he asked the globe.

There was a murmur among the giants as Mister Lewis picked up the globe. They nodded at each other and started to close ranks.

"If I did that to your..." Mister Lewis fumbled for which word to use, "mother... do you really want to find out what gifts I brought for you?"

The giants paused, once more glancing at each other.

"Fly away before I change my mind," Mister Lewis bellowed with as much venom as he could muster, and thrusting his left hand in his coat pocket menacingly.

The giants paused and glanced around. Shoulders shrugged and they changed their forms to that of flies. At which point Mister Lewis pulled his left hand out of his pocket. It held a small aerosol can of bug spray. When the giants turned into flies, they really turned into flies. The neurotoxin did its work and they dropped to ground, no longer among the living. Perhaps Loki had been honest about their brains developing more slowly.

Mister Lewis found a dustpan and broom, swept up the flies and flushed them down a toilet. As he left the bathroom, the visibly confused campaign staff were starting to move again. He found the Deputy Director waiting for him outside the building.

"It's done," asked the Deputy Director.

"No one will find any trace of those candidates, but somebody might still vote for them if they're still on the ballots."

"It's easy enough to leave them off the ballots if they're not there to protest," said the Deputy Director. "What about the ringleader?"

Mister Lewis removed the globe from his pocket and showed the Deputy Director. Loki did not look happy.

"Trapped in this orb, which I'll send somewhere unpleasant. I was thinking maybe Antarctica."

"Will it hold him," asked the Deputy Director.

"For a time."

"Is that dangerous for you?"

"We already had a problem," replied Mister Lewis. "This just makes us even. I'm not so sure he doesn't like the abuse. He's a god, so he's used to having time and boredom on his hands, whereas I'm a mortal, so time is money for me. Besides, with a drowned god on my resume, I can probably raise my fees."

9 780974 959856